'Ordinary couple? Who are you kidding? We aren't ordinary. And we aren't a couple!' Francesca exclaimed.

This did not faze Conrad one bit. 'We could be. And nobody's ordinary if you think about it. All you have to do is come with me to official functions. There's about three in the rest of the year. I'll let you have some notes nearer the time.'

'Great. Parties with briefing notes,' muttered Francesca. 'You're sure that's all I have to do?'

'Anything else is entirely up to you.'

Born in London, **Sophie Weston** is a traveller by nature, who started writing when she was five. She wrote her first romance recovering from illness, thinking her travelling was over. She was wrong, but she enjoyed it so much that she has carried on. These days she lives in the heart of the city with two demanding cats and a cherry tree—and travels the world looking for settings for her stories.

Sophie Weston's novels are well-known for whisking the reader away to exciting exotic locations. And the sparks are guaranteed to fly when her lively, contemporary heroines take on men of the world!

Readers are invited to visit Sophie Weston's website at www.sophie-weston.com.

Recent titles by the same author:

THE ENGLISHMAN'S BRIDE
MORE THAN A MILLIONAIRE
THE BRIDESMAID'S SECRET
THE MILLIONAIRE'S DAUGHTER
MIDNIGHT WEDDING
THE SHEIKH'S BRIDE

THE PRINCE'S PROPOSAL

BY
SOPHIE WESTON

First published in Great Britain 2002
Harlequin Mills & Boon Limited,
Eton House, 18-24 Paradise Road, Richmond, Surrey TW9 1SR

© Sophie Weston 2002

ISBN 0 263 83010 1

Set in Times Roman 10 on 11 pt.
02-0602-53214

Printed and bound in Spain
by Litografia Rosés, S.A., Barcelona

CHAPTER ONE

'TODAY,' said Francesca Heller forcefully, 'has been the worst day of my life.'

She was still rather pale. But, being Francesca, she was already fighting back. Jazz decided that the fight needed support.

'Sure it was. So now you show Barry de la Touche that he can't get you down. What better way than to go out and have a good time?

Francesca looked at her in disbelief. 'You can't expect me to go to a party after that.'

Jazz shook her marvellous head of tiny black plaits and refused to back down.

'Yes, I do. You're a professional bookseller now. You go to a publisher's party if it kills you.'

Francesca glared. Jazz was tall, black and gorgeous but Francesca had a glare that would cut steel when she put her mind to it.

Francesca was *not* tall. She was small and slim with ordinary brown hair and an ordinary, pleasant face. 'Invisible in a crowd,' said Francesca's elegant mother with resignation, and Francesca agreed.

But they both underestimated the impact of her eyes. They were huge, wide-spaced and golden brown, fringed with long, sooty lashes. And they *spoke*. Whatever Francesca might say she was feeling, you could see the truth of it in those toffee-brown eyes. Even masked, as they normally were, by big-framed glasses.

Currently she was feeling put-upon. But Jazz Allen was her partner in London's newest independent bookshop, The Buzz. Jazz knew what she was talking about.

'You're not serious,' Francesca said. But without much hope.

'Yes, I am.'

Jazz unwound her long legs from the top of the ladder from which she had been restocking 'Crime, authors F to G,' and slid to the ground.

'But you were here,' said Francesca in despair. 'You *saw*.'

Jazz grinned. 'Your father's got a temper on him,' she said with relish. 'So?'

Francesca stared at her. Jazz had the reputation of being tough. But this was armour-plated.

'Hello?' she said. 'We didn't split off onto different planets this afternoon, did we? You did see my father walk in and demolish the man I thought I was going to marry?'

'I saw your father lob a few firecrackers,' said Jazz serenely. 'But you were never going to marry that twerp.'

Francesca shook her head. She had not confided in Jazz but when she left home that morning she had made up her mind to accept Barry's proposal.

She said desolately, 'I meant to.'

They were supposed to be going out to dinner at one of their favourite restaurants this evening. Francesca had been fondly imagining the candlelit scene. She had even cast the Italian owner to bring out champagne and his concertina while all the other diners applauded. And Barry de la Touche would take her hand, hook her glasses off her nose and look straight into her eyes, in that way he had.

'My bird,' he would have said. And then, 'We were meant for each other.'

But that was this morning's fantasy. And then her father had walked in.

It had been one of Barry's days for working in the stock room. He and Peter Heller had come face to face. Barry, as she could have foretold, was completely outgunned. Peter Heller had been a fifteen-year-old entrepreneur when he escaped from Montassurro. He had survived, and ended up a multimillionaire, by ferreting out his opponents' weaknesses. Then going for the jugular. Barry didn't have a chance.

Her father had produced a string of offences—petty-criminal convictions, a dubious name change, even old school reports. And pointed out that Barry had only started his heavily romantic campaign after he had researched her wealth on the net.

Francesca had not believed him. Well, not at first. But then Peter Heller had announced that he was disinheriting her and Barry's romantic attachment dissolved. Fast. Taking with it a whole raft of Francesca's dreams and most of her self-respect.

But no one would believe that, of course. Everyone thought Francesca was such a fighter.

Now Jazz was bracing. 'You would have thought better of it eventually. There was nothing to Barry, after all. Just Bambi eyelashes and a good story.'

After the scene when her father had flung his accusations at Barry, Francesca could not really take issue with that. She bit her lip.

'Why didn't I see that?'

'You did really,' said Jazz comfortingly. 'Your father may have done the research. But the demolition was strictly down to you.'

Francesca's eloquent eyes widened and widened. She sat down rather hard.

'Think about it,' advised Jazz, seizing a pile of new stock and leaping nimbly up her ladder again to 'Crime, authors H to J'.

Francesca stared blindly at a pile of giraffe-shaped bookmarks that complemented the latest toddlers' book.

She had stood up to her father. She had linked her arm through Barry's and defied Peter Heller for the manipulative, money-grubbing troglodyte that he was. Only Barry was having none of it.

'My bird,' he said tenderly. He drew the glasses off her nose and slid them into his pocket, one of his more charming little tricks, Francesca always thought. It had cost her a fortune in replacement glasses, which she now had strewn about his flat and hers, 'I can't do this to you.'

He kissed her forehead. It was clearly meant to be a gallant renunciation.

Peter Heller snorted. Francesca felt sick.

Without her glasses Francesca could only see a blur. 'We're both young. Healthy. Why do we need my father's money? We can work,' she said in a level voice. 'I don't care what you've done in the past. I'll stand by you. We can make it together—'

And that was the point when Barry turned on her, all charm wiped. She couldn't see him properly. But she could feel it in the jagged movement; hear it.

'No, we can't.'

Peter was delighted. He snapped his fingers. 'Aha!'

Francesca ignored him. She said to the Barry-shaped shadow lowering over her, 'I don't need money—'

'But I *do*.' It was a cry almost of anguish. 'Don't you understand? I've done my time wondering where the next meal is coming from. I'm never going back to that.'

Francesca said nothing.

'Goodbye, Mr Trott,' said Peter. That was Barry's real name. Not de la Touche, after all.

Francesca ignored him. 'You mean you don't think I can afford you,' she said to Barry. Even to herself her voice sounded odd.

'That old bastard has just made sure of that.'

That was when she gave up. That was when she realised this was the end. And this was the worst day of her life.

She gave a little laugh that broke in the middle. 'Yes, I suppose he has.' She held out her hand politely, in the general direction of his voice. 'Goodbye, Barry.'

She was less polite to her father.

And then she went off to the stock room and sought out her absolutely last pair of emergency glasses.

They were in the first-aid box. Their loose arm had been taped up with whatever had come to hand. It looked as if it had been a plaster originally, though it was difficult to tell. It had turned grey in the first-aid box and was fraying elastic bobbles by now. It kept catching on her hair, making her eyes water. That had to be what it was. Francesca, after all, never cried. As her mother always said, she was too like her father to cry.

So now Francesca blinked hard and said to the witch on the ladder, 'What do you mean—the demolition was down to me?'

Jazz looked down at her affectionately. 'Because you didn't tell Barry that you are rich in your own right.'

Francesca jumped. 'What do you mean?'

'Have you forgotten? You told me. When we were first talking about you coming into business I told you I was worried about asking anyone to invest in The Buzz who couldn't afford to lose money. I believe in it—but I could be wrong. And anyway it will take a long time to make a reasonable return on the investment. Let alone get its money back. And you said, ''My father settled a lot of money on me when I was a teenager. It's mine. I can do what I like with it.'' So I said, OK, then, let's go for it. Don't you remember?'

Francesca swallowed. 'Yes. Yes, I do now. I see.'

'So when you said Peter couldn't disinherit you, that was the literal truth, wasn't it? He's already handed over your inheritance. Why didn't you explain that to Barry?'

'I—tried.'

'No, you didn't,' said Jazz shrewdly. 'You wanted to know too. Didn't you, Franny?'

'Know?'

'Whether the money was important to him or not.'

Francesca flinched. But she was a woman who faced the truth, however unpleasant. Truth was important. 'I suppose so.'

'See? You weren't *completely* taken in. You had your doubts, like the sensible woman you are.'

'Sensible, unattractive woman,' muttered Francesca.

'You would never have married that idiot—' Jazz did a double take. 'What?'

Francesca made a clumsy gesture. 'Every man who has ever been interested in me was either dazzled by my mother's title or my father's millions.' Truth had taken hold with a vengeance. 'When they managed to focus on me long enough to see what was really on offer they all backed off.'

Jazz was shocked, as much by the resignation in her voice as what she had actually said.

'Nonsense,' she said.

It was just ten seconds too late. Francesca smiled wearily.

'You don't know the disasters I've had, Jazz.'

'Haven't we all? It's called growing up.'

'By twenty-three I should have cracked that one,' Francesca said drily. 'No, I've got a bit missing when it comes to understanding people. Figures, fine. I can do sums standing on my head. Facts, great. I can remember them and I don't muddle easily. But *people*! I'm hopeless and I always have been.'

Jazz could not think of anything to say.

Francesca stood up and squared her shoulders. She even managed a lopsided smile.

'So that means I'd better concentrate on a career, right? So lead me to this damned party.'

Conrad Domitio shook his head at the hundredth canapé and thought wistfully about fresh air.

'How long will this go on?' he yelled at the publicity assistant.

She stepped a little closer to the tanned god in front of her. Tall, hazel-eyed, with an athlete's frame and philosopher's formidable brow, Conrad Domitio had everything. Even his voice was sexy. It made her shiver in spite of the competition from a heavy drumbeat. Her and every other woman at Gavron and Blake, his publishers. Probably every other woman in the room, now she came to think about it.

'Another hour,' she yelled back.

She knew, of course, that it would be longer than that. But Conrad Domitio was impatient with publicity. In her dealings with him she had learned to undersell the full extent of their campaign. So she was not telling him that tonight, after the party, she was under strict instructions to bring him to dinner with the girls. After all, he was not only a hero and handsome as hell, he was a prince. A *prince*.

The publicity department had hardly believed their luck when they found out. 'He's a heck of a good writer, too,' his editor had reminded them. But they had waved that aside. They knew what was important in selling books. And *Ash on the Wind* was going to be their spring number-one seller. She could feel it in her bones.

'An hour?' Conrad looked at his watch. He could take an hour. Just. 'OK.'

It would not be so bad if the walls were not plastered with huge photographs of him, looking like a movie star, he thought. He had never wanted to have those photographs taken. To be honest, he had not really wanted to write the book at all. But the expedition's photographer had taken some amazing footage of the erupting volcano and even more telling photographs of the escaping crater party. Always fair, Conrad acknowledged that they deserved a book. Conrad, an inveterate diarist, had more than half of the story already written.

So he had agreed. He did not regret it. He was even quite proud of the book now that it was done. But he was unprepared for the circus that the publishers seemed to fancy.

So far they had come up with wheezes guaranteed to strike cold horror into the heart of a serious seismologist who wanted to work again. Tonight's publicity handout, for example. It made him sound like an ego-driven control freak. That or a comic-book super-hero. Conrad shuddered inwardly and told himself that he could get through an hour of anything if he had to. And the profits from the book were going to a really good cause.

Which was why, nine months after he had led six weary men out of the dust-filled darkness of the erupting volcano, they were standing here drinking Gavron and Blake's cabernet sauvignon surrounded by six-foot-high photographs of steaming mountains and multi-eyed grasshoppers. The lighting was halfway between a disco and a forest thunderstorm, and the music was frankly jungle drums along the river. There were tables piled with copies of glossy books, *Ash on the Wind,* among them, but it would take infrared binoculars to find them, as Conrad had already pointed out.

He looked at his watch again. He could just about see it in the gloom.

'What do you want me to do?' he asked the publicity assistant.

She waved a hand at the seething, chattering crowd. 'Circulate. Circulate.'

Conrad's mouth twitched. For a moment there, she sounded just like his grandfather, ex-King Felix of Montassurro. He did not say so. Instead he gave one of his expressive shrugs.

'The sooner we've spread the word, the sooner I can get my train back to normality, I suppose,' he said with resignation. 'You go that way, I'll go this.'

They turned their backs on each other and he plunged back into the cavernous lighting to do his duty.

The disco lighting shook Francesca out of her shell-shock. Well, a little.

'I should have changed,' she said, watching a woman in a strappy silver top flit past, waving.

Jazz grinned after the woman. 'Party organiser,' she diagnosed. 'Don't worry about it. Half the people here will have come straight from work like us. The only people in combat gear will be authors and the younger editors.' She surveyed Francesca and made an unwelcome discovery. 'Oh, no. Not the first-aid-box glasses.'

Francesca was defiant. 'They're all I could find.'

Jazz held out her hand. 'Give them here.'

'But I'm as blind as a bat without them. You don't know what it's like to be as short-sighted as I am.'

'I'll read the instructions to you,' said Jazz without sympathy. 'Try to get a drink and not bump into the furniture.

That's all you need tonight. Get a business card off anyone who sounds worth following up.'

'But—'

'No serious businesswoman is going to work a room like this with bandaged glasses.' And, as Francesca muttered rebelliously, 'You're going all out for the career, remember?'

'I'd still like to be able to see.'

'No,' said Jazz with finality. 'You're representing The Buzz tonight. We're hip. We're cool. Bandaged glasses aren't.'

Francesca gave in and surrendered her glasses. Jazz picked up a glossy bag and handed it to her.

'Publicity handouts and party favours. Take what you want. Lose the rest.'

Francesca was rueful. 'I've got a lot to learn.'

Jazz was already flicking through the bag's contents. 'Chocolates,' she said with satisfaction. 'Keep them. Party programme. Need that. Now, what books have we? *Spot the Whale.* Nah. *Five Thousand Years of Refuse.* The definitive story of trash by Professor Somebody. That will pull the punters in. Not. *Ash on the Wind.* Two authors. I don't like that. Still, they both look quite tasty. Let's see.'

Francesca knew it was hopeless to try and read anything without her glasses. In that dark party room she was going to do quite well if she managed not to walk into something.

'I'm going to be a hazard to shipping tonight,' she said drily. 'Curse all serious businesswomen and their image problems.'

But Jazz was not paying attention.

'Hey. Look at this,' she said excitedly. She stuffed a shiny sheet into Francesca's hand, scanning the entrance hall avidly.

Francesca squinted at a moody black and white photograph. There seemed to be a face in there somewhere. She gave it back. 'Sorry.'

'He's yummy,' said Jazz, seizing the handout impatiently. 'But he's a lot more than that. Listen.'

She read the publicity blurb aloud.

'"Conrad Domitio is one of the best seismologists of the age. But he is not a vulcanologist. When he went along on Professor Roy Blackland's expedition to Salaman Kao it was his first venture into a volcano's crater.'"

'Oh, not another volcano book!'

'Listen,' said Jazz, rapidly skimming the handout. 'This is the good bit.

'"For Conrad Domitio is also known as Crown Prince Conrad of Montassurro. He is heir to his grandfather, the seventy-five-year-old ex-King Felix. Felix himself fled to London via Italy, having spent his teenage years fighting assorted invaders from the Domitios' impregnable fortress in the mountains. Ex-King Felix has no doubts. 'My grandson is a born leader,' he says.

'"To Conrad Domitio himself the answer is simple. 'I was doing everything by the book because I was new,' he said. 'The others were just too used to the conditions. But I'd only just finished reading up everything about volcano eruptions. So I still remembered the *Idiots' Survival Guide*.'

'"Six men are alive today because he did. This is their story.'"

She looked up.

'Montassurro?' said Francesca. She pulled a face.

Jazz ignored that. 'Body of Apollo, and he saves lives too,' she said with relish. 'Cool, huh?'

Francesca shrugged. 'I should think he took charge because he expects people to jump when he says jump. They were a hard lot, the Montassurran royals.' She did a double take. 'How do you know *what* sort of body he has?'

'I looked,' said Jazz calmly. 'He's over there. Tall guy, navy shirt, buns to die for. You're probably the only woman here who didn't clock him the moment she got here.'

Francesca flung up her hands in a gesture of surrender. 'All right. All right. I'm sorry about the glasses. What else can I say?'

'It's not just the way he looks,' said Jazz throatily. She cast a languorous look across the room. 'I want him. Get him for me.'

Francesca shook her short brown hair vigorously. 'Get him yourself,' she retorted. 'What am I? A retriever?'

'You're the one in charge of book signings and evening talks,' pointed out Jazz smugly. 'And this is your subject. Go and make him an offer he can't refuse. The man's a dish.'

Francesca gave her a wicked grin. 'Dishes are your department. I just do figures and boring science books. And I can't even *see* the man.'

'At least that means you'll keep your hands off him. By the look of it, that will have rarity appeal tonight,' said Jazz drily.

Francesca tried not to wince. 'You want him, you do the luring,' she said firmly.

Jazz laughed aloud and stopped smouldering in the man's direction. 'I wish. That man is going to be hot, hot, hot. The publishers wouldn't be interested in a new independent like us. They'll concentrate on the big book chains.'

'Well, he doesn't have to do everything exactly as his publisher says, does he?' demanded Francesca, revolted. 'Is he a man or a mouse?'

'He's a writer who wants to sell his book,' said Jazz practically. 'If the publisher's PR people tell him to paint himself green and juggle babies, he'll do it. He wouldn't look at us. It's hopeless.'

Francesca was not a pushy person. But she was sufficiently her father's daughter to dislike being told anything was hopeless. And Barry had dented her ego as well as her heart.

Well, there was not much she could do about a broken heart, she thought. It would just have to heal in its own time. But all the ego needed was to go all out for something—and get it, of course. Tonight was not her night for being a good loser.

'Oh, won't he?' she said militantly.

Jazz watched with well-disguised satisfaction as she

plunged into the crowd in the general direction of the Crown Prince of Montassurro. Even without her glasses, there was a reasonable chance that she would connect with him, thought Jazz. Three months of working together had taught her that Francesca on a mission was nearly unstoppable. She smiled, well-pleased with her strategy.

Francesca set off on a spurt of pure adrenalin. It took barely three steps for it to wear off.

She was too small for this sort of crowd, she thought wryly. She tried to suppress the urge to keep jumping for air. It felt as if everyone was twice as tall as she was. Taller and more confident and a whole lot more knowledgeable. And all talking over the top of her head.

'So what else is new?' muttered Francesca, unheard. She pinned on a bright, impervious smile.

Exit adrenalin. Enter pure will power. I can do this thing. And then maybe, just maybe, this won't be the worse day of my life after all.

She plunged into the drum-filled darkness.

It was like searching for extraterrestrial intelligence. Of those that managed to hear her shouted enquiry, no one knew where Conrad Domitio was, even if they recognised the name. Most of them were having too good a time even to pretend that they were interested.

Francesca cursed all crown princes and paused to take stock.

Then, 'Did you say Domitio?' said a tall man behind her.

She swung round. And had to look up. And up.

It was too dark to make out much, of course, even if she had not been missing her glasses. But she had the overwhelming impression of strength. More than strength.

She blinked and said in a little confusion, 'Yes. Do you know him?'

The man hesitated.

Francesca tried to focus her eyes. It was hopeless. But there was something about the man that made her really want to *see* him. Ridiculous, of course.

She shook her head and said with determined practicality, 'Because if you do I really want to talk to him.'

The man bent towards her. 'What?'

She caught a hint of some outdoorsy smell, cedar or wood smoke, faint as a half-forgotten memory. And as powerful. She was taken aback. When had she last noticed a stranger's scent? It made her feel somehow feral, animal in a way she did not quite like.

He took her elbow. 'Let's go somewhere where we can hear ourselves talk.'

He took her out onto a small balcony. The dark, seething room fell away like a suffocating cape. It was raining but an awning kept the worst of it off them. And he turned her towards him.

An impression of strength? She must have been out of her mind. This man had more than strength. He was like rock. Warm, magnetised rock. And he knocked all the breath out of her just by being there. Something inside began to vibrate, imperceptibly, in response to that magnetism.

'Cold?' he asked.

Francesca shook her head. She did not trust herself to speak.

His voice sent little trickles of awareness up and down her spine. It startled her. She did not usually react to complete strangers with that sort of physical response.

This is rebound time. Barry's gone and you haven't had time to find your feet. Don't do anything stupid.

He pushed the glass door shut behind them. The party noise modified somewhat. The drum throb stayed. So did the abrasive guitars. But the conversation died down to a background hum.

Even without her glasses, she could make out the way he moved. It was slow, smooth as oiled machinery, almost lazy. And yet there was such purpose there. Yes, definitely an outdoors man, she decided.

And then he turned and said, 'So why are you looking for Conrad Domitio?'

And she felt as if she had walked into a wall.

She stared up at him. Wishing she were taller. Wishing like mad that she was wearing her glasses and the dark features were more than a blur. Wishing that she could be calm. For some reason the adrenalin seemed to be back in charge again. It was making her pulses gallop crazily.

The bright, impervious smile wavered. 'I—I want to invite him to a book signing,' she said literally, shaken.

'A book-signing?' He sounded lazy.

So why didn't he feel lazy? He felt watchful and wary. It was as if there he was, watching and criticising and formulating acute observations right here and now in his head. He was just not going to share them with anyone. It was unsettling. And very, very sexy.

If only I could see his face properly. I'm getting new glasses first thing tomorrow.

'Er—yes.' Francesca made valiant attempts to pull herself together. Except for a slight ringing in the ears she managed it, too. 'I'm a bookseller.'

She realised quite suddenly that it was the first time she had said it. It felt good. She stood taller and her pulses slowed a little.

'Rather a new bookseller. I bought into an independent bookshop a few months ago.'

'So you're trying to prove your mettle,' he said thoughtfully.

That hadn't occurred to her. 'I suppose so.'

'Is it fun?' He sounded genuinely interested.

She widened her eyes at him. It did not make her see any better but at least it hid the fact that she was as blind as a bat. 'So far.'

'You're very cautious.' He was so close that she could hear the smile in his voice, in spite of the heavy rock beat in the room behind them.

A laugh was surprised out of Francesca. She grinned up at him. 'OK. So far it's a blast. How's that?'

There was an odd pause. She had the impression that he had suddenly become very intent. The temptation to wrinkle up her eyes to bring him into focus was almost overwhelming. I will *not* squint, she told herself fiercely.

'Much more encouraging.'

Someone tried to slide the door open. He shifted, so that he blocked their way out onto the balcony. There was a muttered apology and the door went back into place.

Of course, she couldn't be absolutely sure, not without being able to see his expression. But it felt as if he wanted to talk to her alone. As if he was uninterested in everyone else. And was making sure that nobody gatecrashed their tête-à-tête.

Oh, wow, thought Francesca.

And then caught herself. That was the woman who had just been dumped speaking, right? She was much too mature to get excited because a man backed her into a corner at a party. Even if it was on a balcony under the stars.

'Where is this bookshop of yours?'

'A funny little side-street near the river in Fulham. Our shop was originally a couple of Victorian cottages. Behind the gasworks. You turn left off the King's Road travelling west…'

She gave him precise directions because that was the way she worked. Francesca was nothing if not spot-on accurate. It seemed to amuse him.

He laughed. 'You're not a map-maker, by any chance?'

'I like to get things clear,' she said, slightly shamefaced. 'Sorry.'

'Don't be. It's very useful. I could do with you on my team sometimes. You have no idea the number of people who think that getting you to roughly the right area is good enough.'

Francesca thought of the photographs of mountains and waterfalls she had seen in the entrance area before Jazz confiscated her glasses.

'Are you a geographer?'

'Sort of.'

She clocked the evasion and wondered about it. Was he a rival bookseller trying to tease out her secrets? But what would be the point of that, when he knew she had only been in the field for a few months? She was hardly a candidate for industrial espionage yet. Now, if it had been Jazz— She remembered her self-appointed task.

'Of course, when I say book-signing, I mean more than that really. We are really building a customer community at The Buzz. Evening events, readings, talks, that sort of thing. People are actually phoning us up and asking when the next one is. We might even do something like this. Oh, not the disco atmosphere. But promoting several books on related subjects. It's a great idea!'

She was babbling. She knew it. But she didn't know why. Sure, he was tall but then so was nearly everyone here by her standards. She did not normally find tall people intimidating.

And he wasn't intimidating exactly. Just—well—compelling. There was a quality in his silence that made her talk, too much and too loudly. And all the time she could feel him looking at her, as if there was something going on in his mind that he was not going to tell her about.

Boy, I get perceptive when I haven't got my glasses.

She cleared her throat and said more rationally, 'And what are you doing here?'

She sensed that he made his mind up about something.

'Oh, I'm one of the performing fleas,' he drawled.

She did not think she had heard him aright. 'What?'

'I'm singing for my supper. Or I will be when I'm trotted out to meet the Press in a few minutes' time.'

'Oh, you're a writer,' she said, relieved.

'That's not how I'd put it,' the tall man said ruefully. 'I just got caught by a predatory photographer when I was too weak to say no.'

'Really?' Francesca was sceptical. She did not think this man was ever weak.

He laughed. 'You must have seen the pictures when you came in. Ten-foot-high volcanic eruptions and a leaping wolf that makes everyone take two steps backwards.'

'I missed the wolf,' she admitted.

'Just as well. Nightmare stuff.'

She couldn't imagine him having nightmares either. She did not say so.

Instead she said curiously, 'You sound as if you disapprove.'

'Me? Hey, what have I got to disapprove of? I've written one of the things. I don't have to endorse each and every one.'

She did not believe the disclaimer. 'But...?' she prompted.

'You're sharp, aren't you?' He sounded faintly put out. 'OK, I admit it. I'm not that keen on coffee-table books. I never expected to find myself contributing to one.'

'So why did you?'

'Phew. Sharp and to the point.' No doubt about it, this time he was seriously taken aback. Then he decided to be amused. She sensed it even before he said, 'They offered me a lot of money. OK? Interrogation over?'

'Interrogation over,' she said. But she could not quite get rid of a feeling of disappointment. She would not have expected this man to be persuaded to do something he did not want to just because someone offered him a lot of money, somehow.

'Now you're the one who sounds disapproving,' he said acutely.

Francesca shifted her shoulders uncomfortably. 'It's easy to be puritanical about money when you have enough, I know.'

He looked down at her and she could almost feel that undercurrent of a commentary she could not hear.

'That's very broad-minded of you.' There was an edge to his voice.

She hurried to change the subject. 'And I'm sure your book will be a success. People lap these picture books up for presents. Especially if they're by a blonde in a wetsuit. Or a royal prince, I suppose.'

'Prince?'

'Yes. That's why I wanted to talk to Conrad Domitio. I see from their handout that they've managed to get him to do some *Boys' Own* adventure.'

There was a long, long pause.

'Ah. So that's why you wanted to find him.' He sounded more than disapproving. He sounded downright hostile.

For a moment a faint suspicion occurred to her. But she dismissed it at once. This was no prince, this tall, rangy man with his backwoodsman's prowl and his slow drawl. Besides, all the Montassurrans she knew were small and dark like her father.

'Well, he's an ex-prince, to be honest. But it seems to impress some people,' she said, thinking of the normally cool Jazz's reaction.

'Some people but not you.'

Francesca gave a hiccup of laughter. 'No, not me. But then, I'm a special case.'

'Yeah? No princes need apply?'

She laughed aloud at that. 'I'm not a rabid anti-monarchist, if that's what you mean. I just happen to know a bit about this particular monarchy.'

'Really?' The drawl was even slower than before. And profoundly sceptical.

It flicked her on the raw. She straightened smartly.

'The Crown Prince of Montassurro,' announced Francesca, back in precision-detail mode, 'is pretend royalty from an obscure bit of the Balkans. Couple of mountains, couple of trout streams which they call rivers. Not so much a kingdom, more a family estate.'

There was a faint pause. She certainly had all his attention now.

At last, 'You're very well-informed,' said the backwoodsman lazily.

'I certainly am. Main crops, wine and wheat. Main occupation, brigandage.'

'You've done your research—' He broke off sharply. *'Brigandage?'*

'The Montassurrans in exile run a good story,' said Francesca hardly. 'But basically they have always been a bunch of mountain brigands. Who just happened to settle on the motorway-services station of the Middle Ages. Everyone passing through had to stop there. And pay tribute.'

'That's hardly brigandage.'

'They developed that later. Harried the Turks. Raided the Crusaders. Made a good thing out of kidnap and extortion for about ten centuries. Then got some great PR at the Conference of Vienna and turned themselves into professional freedom fighters.'

There was stunned silence.

Then, 'You sound like an expert,' he said slowly. 'Did you major in Balkan history?'

Francesca gave a snort of laughter. 'In a way. My father came from Montassurro. I grew up on the stories.'

Another, longer silence. She could almost feel him thinking. It was still unsettling. And, even now, when they were clearly at odds, it was still sexy. Blast!

'Not very flattering stories by the sound of it.'

'Well, my father *is* an anti-monarchist.'

'And you've inherited his prejudices,' he said as if that explained everything.

Francesca stiffened. 'Not at all. I don't care about monarchy one way or the other. What I can't bear is a lot of people living in the past. Ex-kings, huh! You can't spend your life as an ex-anything. You have to draw a line and go on.'

'You're very—unforgiving.'

She stared, confused. 'Why? Because I don't like a lot of phoney nostalgia?'

He was looking at her in that way again. She couldn't see him properly but the reservations were coming off him in waves. As if there were two conversations going on and she was only hearing one—and the less interesting one, at that.

Oh, God, here I go again. Listening to the facts. Not hearing the meaning. What the hell is wrong with me?

'Because you think you can draw a line under a bit of yourself and leave it behind.' He was drawling again. 'How old are you?'

Francesca's eyes snapped. 'Twenty-three. How old are you?'

He gave a soft laugh. 'Thirty-two. Going on a hundred, just at this minute.'

'Why this minute?'

But there was no chance for him to answer. The glass door was pushed violently back. Music and revellers spilled out onto the balcony with equal disruptive force. He sidestepped them and took the opportunity to look at his watch.

'I ought to be doing my duty in the Press room.'

'Oh.' She was horribly disappointed and furious about it. Rebound indeed! She curbed it and held out her hand. 'Good luck.'

He took it. 'Will I see you later?'

She shook her head vigorously. As much at her own unwanted fantasies as at him. 'As soon as I've caught up with my prince I'm going home.'

He smiled faintly. She could hear it in his voice. 'Ex-prince.'

And he held on to her hand. It was heady stuff.

'Whatever,' she said, distracted.

'You like to be accurate.'

'Yes.' She was still oddly shaken. 'Yes, I suppose I do.'

'It's obvious. Well, then, we'd better say goodbye.'

He tugged her hand, bringing her a critical step closer to him. Bent—he had a long way to bend—and brushed her cheek with his lips.

Francesca gulped. For a moment she was in a cloud of cold, pure air, surrounded by cedar and a sense of imminent danger, as if she were facing a climb that was beyond her. And then she was on a crowded balcony again on a wet London night. And the stars had gone in.

'Er—goodbye,' she said, more breathless than she would have liked.

He straightened. 'Good luck yourself. I hope you get your ex-prince.'

Francesca, who never gave up on any of her self-appointed

tasks, was for the first time in her life going to pass. She had no intention of doing anything more this evening than going home and trying to get her breath back. But she was not admitting that to anyone else. And, besides, there was always another day. One way or another, she would get the crown prince to one of The Buzz's book-signings if it killed her.

'Cast-iron certainty,' she said, sticking her chin in the air. She was not going to lose focus because Barry de la Touche had dumped her and a tall stranger had not quite kissed her. She was *not*. She said as much to herself as to him, 'I always get my man.'

CHAPTER TWO

'I WANT,' said Conrad, pleasant but very firm, 'to know about a bookshop. It's near the gasworks in Fulham. I'm not moving until I know the name of the woman who owns it.' He looked as if he meant it.

The publicist had been looking for him with increasing desperation. The Press interviews were not going well. The editorial director had called one journalist a freeloader. Then he told a researcher for a daytime television programme that he didn't expect her viewers to be able to read words of more than one syllable. It was definitely time to break out their secret weapon. Only it looked as if the secret weapon had ideas of his own.

'I'll find out for you,' she promised. 'Just please come and talk to the Press *now*.'

'How will you find out?'

'Ask. Someone in this crowd is bound to know.'

'But I don't know the name of the bookshop.'

'Doesn't matter. It's a small world, books.' She urged him towards the room where the Press interviews were taking place. 'What does she look like? How old? What's she interested in?'

'Small. Dark. Huge brown eyes. Sometimes they go all big and misty as if you're the most wonderful thing she's ever looked at. Sometimes they snap. She's twenty-three, and she's fierce.'

'Oh,' said the publicity assistant, rather taken aback. 'Well, that ought to find her. Fulham, you said?'

By the time he had played his part in the discussion of *Ash on the Wind*, she was back.

'Sounds like Jazz Allen's place. It's called The Buzz. But Jazz is nearly six feet, black and beautiful.'

'Not her. Look again.' He thought. 'She also knows a lot about Montassurro. Or thinks she does. Her father was some sort of refugee.'

One of the journalists who had slipped out in the hopes of a private exchange with the ex-prince overheard. He inserted himself between them.

'Do you mean Peter Heller's daughter?'

Conrad's brows twitched together. 'Heller?' he said in tones of acute distaste. 'That crook?'

The journalist grinned. 'Can I quote you? He's an esteemed international financier these days.'

Conrad did not smile. He was looking really disturbed.

'Are you telling me that Peter Heller's daughter would waste her time with a small bookshop? In the shadow of the gasworks? I don't believe it.'

'Not that small,' said the journalist drily. 'Everyone's talking about The Buzz. They've got quite an internet presence already, too. It was the Heller girl who set that up, by what I hear.'

'You mean Jazz Allen's new partner?' said someone else, joining them. 'I hear she's a phenomenon.'

'Yes,' agreed the journalist. 'Everyone thought it was going to be a three-day wonder for her. Well, she's rich enough to invest in a little business like that without caring too much if she gets her money back. But it hasn't turned out like that.'

'You are so right,' agreed someone else, with feeling. 'Francesca Heller is no sleeping partner. My reps say she challenges them all the time. Fearsome woman. But she's certainly improved their ecology list. And Jazz thinks she's wonderful.'

'So does Prince Conrad, from the sound of it,' said the journalist with a sly glance sideways.

But he did not get the response he was hoping for. The tall man looked at him in silence for a moment. The heavy-lidded eyes were quite unreadable. Then he turned away, shrugging.

'Well, would you get the email address for me?' he asked

the publicity assistant indifferently. 'I said I would do a talk
for them some evening.'

He did not say another word on the subject of Francesca
Heller all evening. Instead, to his hosts' surprised delight, he
circulated conscientiously. He even stayed until the very end
of the party.

But, though he got a very good proposition from a giggling
copy editor in low-cut spandex, and the editorial director offered to take him to dinner and throw ideas around about a
series, there was no sign of Francesca Heller. He shook his
head at both invitations.

'No, thanks. Unless—there's no one else left inside, is
there?'

'No. Just us,' said the copy editor, weaving slightly. 'You'd
better come. You'll have missed every last train. Come to the
club with us and then take the milk train at dawn.'

'I'm all partied out, thanks. I'll get a train after breakfast.'

There was consensus that this was a waste.

Conrad's steep eyelids drooped in the familiar bored expression.

'Goodnight, everyone. Have a good one.'

He strolled away. He didn't appear to move fast. But those
long legs had taken him out of sight before anyone could think
of an argument to call him back.

Francesca, Conrad thought.

Odd name for a girl who was half-English, half-
Montassurran. Sounded Italian. Come to think of it, she looked
like one of the Italian beauties you found in Renaissance paintings, all abundant hair and wide pure brow, with their enig-
matic half-smiles. He had always thought they were probably
too intelligent for their own good, those serene, secretive
women. There was always something mysterious about them,
something that said, 'You don't really know me at all.'

Of course, Francesca Heller had not been particularly serene
this evening. But she had not come across as a second-

generation Montassurran confidence trickster either. His jaw tightened.

Not that she thought of herself as Montassurran, obviously. All that nonsense she had talked about brigands! He should have challenged her on it at once. He could not think why he had not.

Hell, yes, he could. He knew exactly why. She had been looking at him with those wide, wide eyes, as if she was somehow caught up in a dream, and all he wanted to do was keep her looking at him like that forever. OK, maybe she was not serene. But the mystery was there all right. By the bucketful.

Fool, he castigated himself. Stupid fool! All she was interested in was catching a prince for one of her bookshop events. She had even admitted it. From all he could find out, she was as good at business as her father. And Peter Heller's daughter was the last person in the world he wanted to tangle with.

Yes, that was better. He would walk a while and think of everything he knew about her father.

Conrad reminded himself that he knew a great deal about Peter Heller and his business dealings. The whole Montassurran community in London did. And they knew Heller was ruthless, acquisitive, and not at all scrupulous. Without actually doing anything criminal, Peter had exploited more than one of the Montassurran exiles who had been so ready to welcome him when he first got to London.

Remember that! Conrad thought. Thinking of Peter, the multimillionaire exploiter, would put mysterious, misty-eyed Francesca Heller in perspective.

Except that it did not. Not quite. She was under his skin, like a rose thorn.

Conrad walked hard, hardly noticing the cold night or the desultory rain. Feet pounding on the pavement, he could convince himself that she was a momentary aberration; that he did not want a woman in his life whom he would be ashamed to introduce to his grandfather and the people his grandfather thought of as his subjects; that he did not want a misty-eyed innocent in his life either, come to think of it. And then he remembered the way her chin came up when she thought he was mocking her. The way her breath caught when he touched her. And the wide, wondering eyes that seemed to look into his very soul.

Look, he said to himself. Either Francesca Heller was what she ought to be as her father's daughter, a real wily operator. In that case she was not the woman for him. Or she was what she had looked tonight. It was a faint outside chance. No woman of twenty-three was so open, so unguarded, so—he said it to himself deliberately—vulnerable. But if she was—

Ah, if she was, then Conrad Domitio was not the man for her.

Francesca gave up soon after the tall man left her. The crowd was too pressing. She couldn't find Jazz. She was never going to find a prince she did not know. Especially if everyone else was after him too. She collected her coat and bumbled out into the rainy dark.

Without her glasses, of course, it was not easy to find a cab. She flagged down a Range Rover, a delivery truck and a traffic light showing amber before she connected with a taxi for hire. She gave the driver the address and then fell back against the upholstery and closed her eyes. Tomorrow morning she was going to order three pairs of glasses—one for home, one for the shop and one for her handbag. This evening's nightmare was never going to happen again.

But it had not all been a nightmare, something whispered. The tall man on the wet balcony. He had not been a nightmare. He had been—exciting.

Yes. Well. There was such a thing as rebound. She had already warned herself once tonight…

That was when it hit her. The difference between expectations and reality—it got you every time. She had expected the evening to end with herself and Barry going back to the riverside flat together. They should have been planning their future. They would have been acknowledged as lovers. She would have belonged somewhere at last.

Instead of which she was sitting alone in the back of a London taxi cab, going through streets she could barely see and certainly not recognise, dreaming about a man she would not recognise if she saw him again.

Well, *probably* not. Though that air of power was pretty impressive. Maybe that would survive, even when she got her glasses back and could actually see the man's face. And that aura of leashed energy, the outdoorsy smell of wood smoke and cedar—she would recognise those at fifty paces.

Francesca realised it with a little shock.

'Wow! Rebound and a half,' she muttered, trying to laugh at herself.

But it wasn't funny. Barry's defection must have left her so vulnerable that she was fantasising about a complete stranger. That was what adolescents did. And Francesca, the world's most self-contained schoolgirl, had not done it, even when it was normal.

'Oh, boy. Postponed adolescence strikes at last,' she said bitterly. 'Francesca, my girl, you have got to be careful. Or this could get out of hand.'

It was not a good night. She tried to go to bed. But she kept thinking of Barry. And the stranger. And Barry again.

There was a nasty moment when she found her second best pair of glasses behind a sofa cushion. She remembered when he had taken them off, between kisses. She remembered what she had thought they would be doing tonight. By now she and Barry would have been stretched out on that sofa. He would have been playing with her hair, teasing her about what he called her twenty-twenty pernicketyness.

'Let yourself go,' Barry would instruct. 'Stop counting. Free the imagination. Fly with me.'

Fly? *Fly?* How on earth had she ever thought she could change? She was never going to fly. She did not have the imagination. And her taste in men was terrible, too. Look at how she only had to close her eyes and she smelled wood smoke…

Forget the man on the balcony. Think about Barry. At least you knew him. Well, nearly knew him.

For now that she was on her own she was remembering all the times Barry had appeared to be dating another girl. When he made his move on Francesca he had explained all those incidents away so easily. Now she thought about it, she realised that he must actually have been running the two of them in tandem. God, but her judgement was awful.

She gave up on sleeping and swished round the empty flat in her long crimson housecoat. Her mother had given it to her for Christmas. She did not like it. It was too dramatic. But it was almost the only thing in her wardrobe that Barry had not seen.

Her eyes leaked tears. She brushed them away furiously. She never cried, she reminded herself bitterly.

She was not missing him. She had never known him, so how could she be missing him? What she was missing was tenderness. Well, the illusion of tenderness. No man in his right mind would really feel tenderness for a woman who found it easier to add up than let her imagination fly. Who inherited her looks from a father who looked like a troglodyte. Who wore glasses held together with a grubby plaster.

Even the stranger would not have wanted to talk to her if it had not been too dark to see her face.

No, no, in the race for emotional fulfilment she was a nonstarter. And she had just proved it for about the tenth time in her adult life.

'Get used to it,' said Francesca aloud. 'Concentrate on the career. At least you have a chance of getting *that* right.'

So she was already tidying the tables of books when Jazz arrived the next morning.

'I'm sorry, I didn't get you your prince,' Francesca announced, even before Jazz had unwound her rainbow scarf. 'I couldn't find him.'

Jazz extracted a large latte from a paper carrier bag and eased off its plastic lid. She passed it across. After three months she and Francesca knew exactly how the other liked her coffee.

'I'm not surprised,' she said philosophically. 'I managed to chat up Maurice Dillon. He's going to do a workshop for new writers for us next month. What about you? Find anyone interesting?'

Francesca shook her head. 'Only a man who wanted to go out onto the balcony and talk in the rain.'

Jazz raised her elegant eyebrows. 'Sexy.'

To her surprise, Francesca flushed slightly.

'Hey, you didn't do anything I would have done, did you?' Jazz said, amused.

'Of course not,' said Francesca, uncharacteristically flustered.

Jazz laughed aloud.

'I didn't mean that. Well, I did, but— Stop laughing at me. Hell, what do I know what you would have done?'

Jazz sipped her own double espresso. 'Not a lot on a wet night in the open air, to be fair,' she admitted. She sent Francesca a thoughtful look. 'It must have been freezing.'

'Er—yes. Maybe. I—um—I didn't really notice.'

'Ah.' Jazz sipped more coffee. 'So how long did you stay out there?'

'I don't remember.' A hint of defiance had crept into Francesca's voice.

'Ah.' Jazz sucked her teeth. 'Fanciable, I take it?'

Francesca thought about warm magnetism and alien lips brushing her cheek. She could not help herself. She gave a little shiver. It was purely involuntary. And she knew Jazz saw it.

'Fair to middling,' she said, unconvincingly. 'Well, what I could see of him, which was about as defined as a Rorschach inkblot. Which reminds me—can I have my spare glasses, please?'

Jazz did not say anything.

'Look, you can't think I was seriously attracted. Not to someone I only met once.'

'Attraction is usually instantaneous,' pointed out Jazz mildly. 'Not a lot you can do about it. OK, you can choose whether you go with it or not. Spend the night. Or hold out for the whole white wedding with pageboys and bells. That's the stuff you get to take decisions about. Attraction just hits you.'

Francesca shivered again. Even her feelings for Barry had not just hit her. Not in the way that Jazz meant. Not the way they hit other people. Barry had had to tell her that she fancied him, laughing. 'You're such an innocent,' he had said tenderly.

She folded her lips together. 'Not me,' she said quietly.

Jazz was unimpressed. 'Which bad fairy came to your christening and gave you immunity?'

'Listen,' said Francesca intensely. 'Until yesterday I thought I was in love with Barry. I'd made up my mind to marry him, for heaven's sake. I'm not in the market to be hit by attraction.'

Jazz grinned maddeningly.

'What?' yelled Francesca, frustrated. *'What?'*

Jazz wiped the smile off her mouth. It stayed everywhere else, though. 'Whatever you say.'

'Give me my glasses,' said Francesca haughtily. 'I have work to do.'

Jazz did. Francesca stamped off into the stock room, muttering.

Eventually Jazz wandered in after her. 'I know you didn't get hold of this prince last night,' she said. 'But I really think we could do an exciting panel one evening, if we could get him along.'

Francesca had not forgiven her yet. She pushed her glasses up her nose and sniffed. 'Cheap sensationalism!'

'Yes, that's what I thought,' said Jazz equably. 'But I looked at his book last night. Have you read it?'

Francesca stuck her nose in the air.

'Thought not. Well, it's a hell of a story as well as being good popular science.'

'So?'

'So call him—talk to him—tell him how great our customers are—sell him The Buzz.'

Francesca forgot that she had told the stranger last night that she was going to do exactly that. 'Why should I?'

Jazz was prepared for that. She whipped out a glossy laminated sheet of paper from behind her back.

'Take a look at that,' she said impressively.

Francesca stared. This time she could actually see the photograph. It was beautifully composed in moody black and white. It would have made anyone look spectacular. But in this case the photographer had had plenty to work with.

It was an impressive face. Not classically handsome. Not even mildly good-looking. It was too strong for that, with its high cheekbones, prominent crooked nose and heavy-lidded light eyes. But it was a face you wouldn't lightly forget.

Francesca had one instant thought: I wouldn't like to get on the wrong side of him. She shivered, inexplicably.

She turned the sheet over. In addition to the blurb there was another photograph. From the book this time, and in glorious colour, it showed off the man's spectacular tan. He was posed—hell, not even posed—he was standing in a vertiginous landscape. His shirt had clearly lost most of its buttons. It was open and falling off one tanned shoulder as he brandished an axe above his head, laughing. The snow-covered peaks behind him should have made him look small. They didn't.

It was not just that Conrad Domitio was unexpectedly tall. Or even that the strongly muscled shoulders looked as if they could shift Stonehenge if they had to. Lots of men were tall and broad-shouldered. It was the lazy confidence. The mobile, knowledgeable mouth. And the laughter in the steady, steady eyes.

Francesca thought suddenly, *I can't deal with a man with eyes like that.*

Jazz did not share her reservations. 'He's every woman's dream,' she said practically. 'And men are all going to want to be like him. He seems to have got that volcano party down single-handed.' She read aloud,

'"Why was it the new kid on the block who took charge? Was it because of rivalry among the others? Most of them had known each other for years and competed for academic honours. Was it because he was younger and fitter? Conrad is thirty-two and a regular rock climber who swims daily. Or was it because he is genetically programmed to take charge?"'

Francesca told herself to stop the adolescent palpitations and get real. This was nonsense and every atom of her experience told her so.

'"Genetically programmed to take charge!"' she snorted. 'Ludicrous! He's just a bossy guy who's used to throwing his weight about.'

'He saved a lot of lives doing it,' Jazz pointed out. 'And the book's very accessible.'

Francesca turned the sheet back over and looked at the moody photograph.

'So is the author, by the looks of it.'

Jazz bit back a smile. 'Oh, I do hope so,' she said with a languishing look.

Francesca narrowed her eyes to slits. 'You can stop right there. You're not going to wind me up, so don't try it. You don't give two hoots about princes. Not even a sexy article like this.'

Jazz stopped languishing and laughed. 'If he gets the royalty-magazine readers buying real books, I give plenty of hoots,' she said drily. 'And they're the ones we can never get in through the doors.'

Francesca groaned.

'He can write,' Jazz wheedled. 'Oh, boy, can he write. And this is a tough time of year for us. We could really use an Evening with Prince Charming, Franny.'

Francesca sighed. But she did not wriggle any longer. 'OK. I'll ring the publisher.'

'I told you. They won't look at us. We're too small. You'll have to get to him direct. Go on a charm offensive.'

'Charm? Me?' Francesca snorted. 'Dream on!' She thought. 'OK, if the publisher won't come through I'll get on to the Montassurran network and see how much he costs.'

Jazz boggled. 'Costs?'

'Rent-a-Royal,' said Francesca cynically. 'How do you think these ex-royals earn their crust? They hire out their only asset.'

Jazz peered over her shoulder at the strong face in the photograph. 'Would you say his *only* asset?' she murmured wickedly.

Francesca was lofty. 'You have a very low lust threshold.'

'Me? Nonsense. Everyone knows I'm picky, picky. You're the one that's odd. Getting yourself all fogged up by Barry de la Touche!'

Francesca flinched. 'Go on, rub it in, why don't you?' she muttered.

'I can't *believe* that you were really thinking of marrying him.'

Francesca had had a bad night, thinking about just that point. Half the time she could not believe it herself. The other half she remembered him saying caressingly, 'My little bird,' and could believe it all too easily. And, if she was falling for an elusive hint of wood smoke, all the indications were that she could do it all over again. Get a grip, she told herself fiercely. Get a grip.

'All that shows is that I have no discrimination and an excessively gullible response to tenderness,' she said savagely.

Jazz shook her head. 'Why didn't you say something? I could have told you what a phoney he was.'

'Could you?' Francesca was not entirely glad to hear that. 'On the principle that anyone who fancied me had to be a con man?'

'On the principle that, for an alleged playwright, he never

put pen to paper,' retorted Jazz. 'I never knew that he claimed to fancy you. You both kept it very quiet.'

Francesca looked away. 'Barry's idea,' she muttered. 'He said it was bad form to date people you work with. I—well, I've never really worked anywhere for long enough to find that one out. I believed him.'

Jazz swore under her breath.

'Oh, well.' Francesca was determinedly bright. 'I suppose I should look on it as a learning experience.'

Jazz scrutinised her expression. 'Did you really care for him?'

There was a pause.

'I thought so,' Francesca said at last in a low voice.

The normally cool Jazz kicked a waste-paper basket viciously. 'Toad!'

Francesca was touched. 'Hey, I'll get over it.' She rallied. 'Enough learning experiences like this and I'll end up normal.'

And thought, If only that were true!

As Jazz predicted, the publishers were unhelpful. More than unhelpful. The publicity assistant did everything but laugh down the telephone at her request.

'His Highness really has no room in his diary for any more personal appearances,' she announced.

She did not say that she wished His Highness had been persuadable to do any personal appearances at all.

So Francesca had to fall back on Plan B. She was not very happy about it. After her father had inserted himself so dramatically into her love life she had told him exactly what she thought of him and refused to see him, on principle. Actually, she had been very dignified until he had said, 'But I was right. I am always right.' At which point she had lost her rag and told him to get back to New York and not bother about next year's Christmas present.

So to call him and ask his help to contact the Montassurran royals was a real climb-down. She only talked herself into doing it after reminding herself that he had never had any time for the monarchy. He had said so publicly more than once. So he would not be able to introduce The Buzz management to the royal family himself. He would have to pass her on to a friend of a friend of a friend. If he could help at all.

So she called him.

Peter Heller had not gone back to New York but he was clearly at lunch. Somewhere expensive, thought Francesca, hearing the echo of vaulted ceilings as glass and cutlery clinked. Still, that went without saying. Her father enjoyed his wealth with enthusiasm.

'Hello, Dad,' she said, struggling to forget their last encounter. 'How are you?'

'Francesca,' he said, pleased. 'So you have forgiven me for being right.'

Francesca gave up the struggle. 'Thank you, I'm well,' she said coldly, in reply to the question he should have asked. She became as direct as he was. 'I need a favour.'

'Ask. But ask quickly. I have a guest.'

She cut out all explanation. It reduced her request to a single sentence. There was silence.

'You want to meet Prince Conrad?' said her father slowly.

You want an explanation, you ask for it, thought Francesca vengefully. 'Yes,' she said aloud.

Another, longer pause. She heard a waiter murmur something; her father's clipped assent; the sound of wine being poured into crystal. She maintained stubborn silence.

Then her father said abruptly, 'I can arrange that. I will be in touch later.'

And cut the connection before Francesca could even say thank you. Probably just as well in the circumstances, she admitted wryly. She knew she ought to be grateful. But, as always, her father's high-handed commands left her fuming. Still, she wanted his help and he had agreed to give it. Think positive, she told herself.

She would not have been so philosophical if she had seen her father after he snapped his digital phone shut and slid it into his jacket pocket.

He sat back in the generous carver chair and beamed across the table. He looked, thought his elderly luncheon guest, like a cat who had found its way into a cream plant. The guest was not used to it. It made him uneasy. He looked over his shoulder, as if expecting the heavy mob to materialise from the Ritz's impeccable kitchens.

His troglodyte host gave him a wide, wide smile. He leaned forward.

'Now, have I got a deal for you...'

'No,' said Conrad Domitio firmly. 'Absolutely not.'

He had been taking a stand against his grandfather's wackier schemes ever since he was twelve. Experience had taught him that you had to say no early and keep on saying it. Any hint of negotiation and you were lost.

'But you haven't even heard my idea,' said his grandfather. His squashed toad's face managed to look both hurt and hopeful at the same time.

His tall grandson looked down at him with a good deal of understanding. The wind whipping across the urban playground raised Felix Domitio's thin hair. He shivered. Conrad fished some gloves out of the back pocket of his tracksuit and passed them across. But he did not relent.

'I don't need to,' he said, ever rational. 'You got out of bed before eight on a wet Saturday morning to blag me into it. That means you know I won't agree willingly.'

'You are so suspicious,' mourned his grandfather. He pulled the gloves on and stamped his feet a bit to warm them. His highly polished shoes were not designed for the puddle-strewn concrete. They seemed to be letting in water.

'Learned from experience,' said Conrad drily.

He had a dark, secretive face. But, during these Saturday sessions, most of the time it looked as if it was on the edge of laughter. Just at the moment, it had tipped over the edge into outright amusement.

Amusement, Felix Domitio knew, did not bode well for his

grand design. He banished thoughts of a warm fire, at least for the moment.

Instead he folded his newly gloved hands over his old-fashioned waistcoat and said virtuously, 'But it's such a good cause.'

'Sure it is. That's why I'm going out to Montassurro with the relief expedition just as soon as we can get that mobile hospital equipped.'

'Well, then, my idea is such a tiny thing to do, in comparison,' said Felix in triumph. 'All you have to do is climb into the Mountain Hussars uniform and be polite to people.'

The dark face hardened. 'You mean prance around like something out of a Strauss operetta wearing a lot of medals I'm not entitled to.'

When he wasn't laughing Conrad Domitio could look quite forbidding, thought his grandfather.

'You're entitled,' he protested. 'I confer them on whomever I want.'

Conrad shook his head. 'You don't understand, do you? All right, Grandad. Medals I didn't earn. Does that make it clearer?'

His grandfather hunched his shoulders pettishly. 'You're such a puritan.'

But Conrad was laughing again. 'Sorry about that.'

Felix huddled his coat round him and stamped his feet some more.

'Take this place, for example,' he said, momentarily distracted. 'You know your aunt offered you the big room in the house at Prince's Gate for your class. You don't have to trail out to a wretched housing estate. So dreary.'

There was a slightly dangerous pause. *I wish I hadn't said that,* thought Felix.

'You need to get out more,' Conrad said at last. But he was not laughing any more. He spoke curtly. 'It's a perfectly OK housing estate. It's where the children live. I teach them the language of their grandfathers. I know why I do it. I'm never quite sure why they do. They would much rather be watching television or playing computer games. If I didn't come to them, if they had to struggle up to central London, it might just tip the balance. And then they wouldn't come. OK?'

Felix backtracked fast. 'Of course, you're right. I wasn't thinking. Put it down to the early morning and wet feet. Now, about the people you need to be nice to. Peter Heller's made me an offer to fund the mountain clinic for the first year—'

There was an odd silence. Felix found Conrad was looking at him in disbelief.

Eventually he said, 'You *do* need to get out more. Heller's as cunning as a fox. He never gives anything for nothing, least of all money.'

But Felix thought that was not the first thing he had intended to say.

'Well, maybe,' he admitted. 'But this time I think he genuinely wants to help the relief effort.'

'No, he doesn't. Peter Heller has never had a disinterested urge in his life.'

The children were beginning to arrive. Conrad greeted them as they passed. He knew everyone by name, Felix saw. Some of the smaller girls gave a quick, shy bob in response to Conrad's smile.

Felix gave a sharp sigh. What a king Conrad would have made, he thought wistfully. So shrewd, so tenacious, such an excellent judge of character. He pulled himself together. Might still make, if things turned out as Felix hoped and planned. As long as he could persuade Conrad, of course.

But Conrad was not thinking about his potential future subjects. Conrad was being as uncooperative as he knew how.

'You can't trust a word Heller says. If he's signing a cheque he'll want a damn sight more for it than a photograph of me in my gold trimmings, shaking his hand.'

Felix's eyes slid away. Fortunately Conrad was looking at a couple of boys who had just arrived and were quartering the playground like secret-service agents, so he did not notice.

'He'll want to make money,' Conrad said, following their progress with hawk-like vigilance. 'What does he think we can do for him? Get him the inside track on the cigarette franchise?'

'Er—no.'

'Well, he'll want something.'

Felix studied the grey sky as if he had just been appointed to the weekend-weather bureau.

'Maybe he's just a patriot,' he suggested to the cloud cover.

Conrad was unimpressed. 'Patriot? Peter Heller? He went through the patriots in London twenty years ago and left most of them poorer. He's a fixer.'

'A rich fixer,' murmured the ex-king ruefully.

'So he backed the right generals.' Conrad shrugged. 'He was a wide boy when he got out of Montassurro all those years ago. And he's a wide boy now. We shouldn't have anything to do with him.'

This was turning out more difficult even than Felix had expected.

'That's why I came over,' he said craftily. 'I really value your advice, you know. When you've heard the rest of my idea—'

But his grandson was one of the few people in the world ex-King Felix of Montassurro could not manipulate.

'No,' said Conrad briskly. 'Whatever the rest of your idea is, the answer's the same. No way. No. Now go away. I have work to do.'

Felix was undeterred.

'No, you don't. The children are perfectly happy.' He waved a hand at the cheerful early-morning buzz.

'That's what worries me.'

Conrad swept the crowded urban school yard with a sector-by-sector surveillance. His eyes were narrowed in concentration. Not just vigilant, he was merciless as a hawk, too.

His eyes came to rest on the secret-service couple. At once the boys shoved their hands in their pockets and looked airily at the sky. Conrad's eyes stayed on them, unwavering. They took their hands out of their pockets and tried hard to disappear into a chattering group.

His grandfather was rather relieved. It was easier to talk to Conrad when he was engaged in a power struggle with playground bullies. Ex-King Felix was not easily deflected from his argument but there was no doubt it was easier to set out your points when your grandson was not taking them to pieces one by one as you did so.

'Think for a moment, my Conrad. What would it cost you?' he said, his accent suddenly pronounced. 'What would it really cost you to do this small thing for your country?'

Conrad did not take his eyes off the cauldron of the playground. 'Don't do your elderly-refugee act with me, Felix. Never forget, I can see the wires.'

His grandfather abandoned the heavy accent. 'All right. But I only want one weekend out of your life. Is that so much to ask?'

'Yes,' said Conrad. 'If it requires me to cosy up to Peter Heller. Absolutely too much.'

His grandfather made East European noises indicative of shock and disappointment.

Conrad looked down at him. He had passed his grandfather in height when he was fourteen. Now he towered over the older man. And it was not just the height that was different. Unlike his grandfather, Conrad had high cheekbones, and unblinking, slanted eyes so dark they were almost black even when he was smiling. They were intimidating, those eyes. He relied on them to keep control of the playground, as much as he relied on his speed of reaction. The only person they had failed to intimidate in the last five years was his grandfather.

Now Conrad said with feeling, 'I'm already kissing goodbye to every Saturday morning. Just so I can teach a lot of kids, who don't want to learn it, a language that they will never use. At least, not unless they manage to get in touch with the ghosts of their great-grandparents.' He added bitterly, 'And I'm not good with kids.'

'Rank has its obligations,' said his grandfather, grinning.

'I'd trade rank for the occasional Saturday morning lie-in.'

'Unfortunately, rank is not a tradeable commodity.'

Conrad flicked up one black eyebrow. 'No?' he said mockingly. 'And there was me, thinking you wanted me to hire myself out as Rent-a-Gent to Heller Incorporated.'

His grandfather snorted. 'You're so sharp you'll cut yourself.'

But suddenly Conrad was not attending. 'Hell, that monster is going to strangle the kid with her own plait,' he muttered. He set off in the direction of the intended mayhem and intensified his voice so that it bounced off the playground walls. 'Gligor!'

An intent ten-year-old looked up, momentarily arrested.

'Don't even think about it,' advised Conrad, arriving.

The ten-year-old narrowed his eyes, assessing the situation with the air of an experienced criminal. Meanwhile a small girl with a plait was sweetly unaware that she had ever stood in any danger; or that it had been averted, however temporarily. But she knew that Crown Prince Conrad had been graciously pleased to approach their group. Her eyes lit up and she broke out a slightly wobbly curtsey.

'Your Royal Highness,' she said, staggering a bit as she came up from the bob.

Conrad sighed and steadied her automatically.

'Why do they do that?' he muttered.

His grandfather came up, rather more sedately.

'You're royal and they do ballet classes,' he said, answering the question literally. 'Put the two together and curtsies become inevitable.'

As if to prove his point, that was the moment at which the small girl identified him. She squeaked, 'Your Majesty,' and sank to the ground, head bowed, red dirndl skirts billowing.

'Now look what you've done,' said Conrad, exasperated.

'Me?' His grandfather was wounded. But he looked down at the small tumble of scarlet skirt and chestnut pigtail that did not rise from the ground. He was a touch disconcerted at this excess of respect. 'Well, well, child, that's enough. Get up now.'

Conrad gave a sharp sigh. 'Don't you see, she's trying?'

And, indeed, the small crouched figure was rocking slightly.

He said patiently, 'It's all right, Dorothea. Hold still for a moment.'

The child stopped rocking obediently.

Conrad picked her up, shook her straight and returned her to her feet. Behind them the ten-year-old delinquent took a step forward.

Without looking round, Conrad said, 'Gligor, leave Dorothea alone.'

The boy paused but not with much conviction.

Conrad swung round and subjected him to his powerful stare. 'If you don't I shall personally extract every tooth in your head with chewing gum and forceps.'

The ten-year-old looked thoughtful.

His Majesty King Felix gave a wistful sigh. 'What a great commander in chief you would make.'

'No, I wouldn't,' said Conrad crisply. 'I make a damn good seismologist and a pathetic occasional teacher. Be content with that.'

'But you are also my heir,' said His Majesty, lapsing into the heavy accent again.

Conrad looked at him. There was a dangerous pause.

But for once Felix did not throw up his hands and admit he was over-acting. He dropped the accent but he said soberly, 'Life is not good in Montassurro. The old order has collapsed and there is nothing to take its place but a bunch of criminals. People are starving, Conrad.'

Conrad said roughly, 'I know. But you've done all you can. Hell, it's not as if the family has even lived there for sixty years…'

His grandfather said simply, 'The Domitio family held the mountains for eight hundred years. I was there myself until…' He broke off.

Conrad knew that his grandfather had roved the mountains with the partisans until he was seventeen. That was when the communists finally took power and Felix had escaped across the mountains to Italy, education and a life of guilty regret.

Conrad put his arm round his grandfather's shoulders. It was a rare gesture.

'We have a duty,' said Felix without any histrionics at all. There was a sharp silence.

'If your father were alive,' said Felix with difficulty, 'I would not ask.'

Conrad made a clumsy gesture. Neither of them ever spoke of Felix's only son. Conrad knew that if his grandfather could bring himself to do it now then this project was more important than anything had been for a long time.

He said wearily, 'OK. You win. I'll come to lunch and be nice to Peter Heller. I'll even listen to what he has to say. But that's where it stops. All right?'

Felix was too experienced a diplomat to rub his hands or jump in the air with glee. He nodded soberly. 'That's good of you, Conrad. Your grandmother will look forward to it.'

But Conrad's antennae were too well-tuned to the family tones. He looked at his grandfather with sudden sharpness.

'That's all I'll do, Felix,' he said warningly. '*Listen.* Absolutely no promises.'

'No promises,' agreed his grandfather. 'But you'll listen. That's all I ask.'

The clock on the nearby church tower started to strike the hour. The children took no notice. Conrad raised his head and let out a cry that the Domitio family had developed when they were calling from peak to peak in the forested mountains.

Most of the children stopped playing and formed a reluctant line at the school door.

The enterprising ten-year-old began to drift casually towards the passageway that led out of the playground. A hand shot out and attached itself to his collar.

'Grammar test this morning, Gligor,' said Conrad, correcting the direction of the child's trajectory. 'Go and clean the blackboard.'

The child recognised superior strength. He went.

'He turned his back on me,' said Felix, displeased. 'He should not turn his back on me. And he should have bowed.'

For the first time that morning Conrad smiled properly. He had a wonderful smile. It lit the opaque eyes like firelight after a snowstorm.

'Look on the bright side, Felix,' he said with pleasure. 'At least he didn't bite you.'

'What?'

'In Gligor's case that's respect amounting to hero worship.'

Felix stared at him in horror. 'This is a joke, right?'

Conrad shook his head, his eyes dancing. 'Literal truth. I've got the scars to prove it. The world has moved on, Felix.' He looked at his watch. 'I'd better get in before they set fire to the place. See you later.'

He did not bow, or back away from the regal presence either, but his grandfather did not complain. His grandfather was too busy hugging himself.

Left alone in the playground, he did a neat soft-shoe shuffle, avoiding a puddle with more agility than might be expected of a man of his years.

'One down,' he told the cool spring morning. 'One to go.'

CHAPTER THREE

'SO TELL me, where exactly are we going?' said Francesca.

She was seated next to her father in the back of a black London taxi. He had told her he was taking her to lunch with an old friend of the family. But then she remembered—it was only her well-connected mother who had friends of the family. Peter had no family, except for an estranged wife and semi-detached daughter. And his friends tended to be, frankly, jet-setting cowboys like himself.

None of her father's usual cronies would have merited silk jersey straight from Paris and heels so high that she had to nerve herself to walk more than a few steps. The outfit was all cream and honey and gold and would need to be dry cleaned after every outing and the shoes nearly crippled her. But her father had had them sent round to the bookshop in great white and gold boxes. 'I want you to look nice,' he said. 'Indulge me.'

Bewildered but touched, she had climbed into the new clothes and organised the rest of the day off. So here she was, looking nice—if acutely uncomfortable—and she still did not know *why*.

And something about her father's demeanour was making her uneasy. He looked out of the window at an elegant regency terrace and hesitated. Francesca's suspicion was increasing exponentially. Her father *never* hesitated.

She swung round on the taxi seat and eyed him beadily. 'Who is it? Come clean, Dad.'

After a moment he did. 'The Domitios.'

She was blank. 'Who?'

'The ex-king and -queen. Felix and Angelika.'

Francesca frowned. She did not know all the details but she

knew her father's relationship with the Montassurran court in exile could best be described as edgy. And it still did not account for that faint air of guilt that she was picking up on her radar.

'I didn't know they were friends of the family.' She watched him narrowly.

'Not so far, perhaps. But I hope we are going to be very good friends in the future.'

He was always very quick on his feet, give him that, thought Francesca, amused in spite of herself. She supposed he was doing some deal in Montassurro. She had seen newspaper suggestions that the ex-king might be asked back to take some role in the strife-torn government.

'OK. So why did you bring me along?'

Peter Heller looked amazed. Just a little bit too amazed, to be honest. Francesca was sure that he had been practising. Also horribly virtuous. 'But you asked me. It was your idea.'

'What?'

'You said you wanted to meet Prince Conrad.'

'Ah,' said Francesca, understanding at last. 'Well, I didn't actually mean formal lunch with the whole regal shooting match. I was thinking of a drink in a pub one night. Or even his phone number would have done.'

Her father was unrepentant. 'Then you should have said so. I have pulled out all the stops to arrange this meeting. I thought it was going to help you.'

'Yeah. Well, I suppose I could try cornering him behind the samovar,' said Francesca doubtfully. She had not had much experience of royalty but the last of her ten schools had specialised in adding social gloss to its pupils. She had never expected all that white-gloves-and-precedence stuff to come in handy. It looked as if she had been wrong. 'Am I going to have to curtsey to anyone?'

That startled him out of his well-rehearsed sanctimoniousness.

'No!' he said with every evidence of disgust.

Francesca sat back in the taxi and hid her grin. That was the father she knew, all right.

'Just checking.'

It was her father's turn to look uneasy.

'I hope you are going to behave.'

She beamed at him. 'I'll just bet you do.'

'Francesca—'

But they had arrived. The taxi stopped outside an impressive Edwardian mansion block. Francesca waved whatever he was going to say away as she cautiously got out of the cab and straightened on her spindly heels. So far, so good, she thought. Though it was just as well her father had vetoed the curtsey. It was not a viable option in four-inch heels.

She pushed her new and fashionable gold–trimmed spectacles up her nose and held tight to his arm as he led the way inside.

'This is going to be a new experience,' she said brightly.

She did not know how right that was going to turn out to be.

Francesca had been to a lot of formal lunches in her time. The menus changed. The venues changed. But there were three things that always stayed the same—huge flower arrangements, acres of napery and massively ceremonial service from frosty-faced waiters in evening dress. She had never before been to a formal lunch party in an overstuffed flat whose décor was somewhere between a throne room and a junk shop. Nor had she ever found the grand hostess setting the table when her guests arrived. There was not a frosty waiter in sight.

'Oh,' said ex-Queen Angelika as her husband ushered the guests into the sunlit apartment.

She was wearing a magnificent ruby pendant and a harassed expression. It did not lighten at the sight of Francesca. In fact, it was invaded by a slight but unmistakeable hint of frost.

Oops, thought Francesca. Should have curtsied after all.

'How nice to meet you at last, Miss Heller. I've heard so much about you.'

Francesca looked wildly at her father. What on earth had

he been saying? But he was shaking hands with the ex-king, and not looking her way. Rather studiously not looking her way.

So she said lightly, 'Oh, dear, that always sounds rather threatening. As if the "Wanted" posters have been put up.'

Her hostess smiled. It was a mere stretch of the brightly painted mouth. Ex-Queen Angelika, Francesca deduced, was not lining up with bouquets to welcome Peter Heller back into the Montassurran fold.

But she said nicely enough, 'Nothing bad enough to have a price on your head.'

'Not bad *enough*? So quite bad, then?'

Francesca sent her father a burning look of reproach. He should have warned her that they were on a fence-mending mission. At least as far as the ex-queen was concerned. The ex-king, who looked like a frog, seemed perfectly happy to welcome Francesca. He didn't seem to want a curtsey either. He shook hands enthusiastically.

Ex-Queen Angelika said sweetly, 'Well, you've never really stuck at anything properly, have you, dear?'

Ouch.

Francesca straightened her shoulders. Whatever she might be willing to admit to herself or Jazz, her friend, she was not taking criticism from some old bat she had just met, queen or no queen.

'I think it's a big mistake to commit yourself too soon,' she said with a glittering smile. 'So I've taken my chance to see the world and experience lots of different things. I have plenty of time, after all.'

Their eyes locked.

Battle joined, thought Francesca, who had not sat through her mother's elegant demolition of social rivals for nothing.

The ex-queen nodded, as if she realised it too.

Francesca relented. She made a gesture towards the half-set table. 'May I help you, perhaps?' she suggested.

There was only the tiniest moment before the ex-queen accepted graciously. The men would not have noticed it, thought

Francesca. But her hostess made quite certain that Francesca did.

'That is very kind. Thank you.' Waving her husband and his guest into the sitting room, the ex-queen said, 'We can have a comfortable chat, woman to woman.'

'Oh,' said Francesca.

Chat, she doubted. Comfortable she was damn certain it would not be. She felt she had been outgunned by a professional.

The ex-queen led the way to the kitchen as if she were entering a full court ball with a lady-in-waiting in tow. Francesca's heart sank even further. She pushed her new glasses up her nose defensively. Thank heavens she had at least managed to get to the optician in the last ten days. She did not think the ex-queen would overlook spectacles held together by a dirty plaster.

She was still thanking her guardian angel for saving her from a royal reprimand when the ex-queen said, 'I understand you are—interested—in my grandson.' She made it sound faintly disreputable.

Francesca flushed. 'Strictly in a business sort of way.'

The ex-queen stiffened. 'You are very forthright.'

'I find it's always easier if you say what you want up front,' said Francesca, wondering what she had said to make the old bat look like that. 'Saves on the misunderstandings.'

'Quite.' The ex-queen's mouth set like a trap. 'Very twenty-first century. No pretence. No courtesies. And heaven forbid that there should be any romance.'

Francesca stared. 'Romance?'

'But I am sure you are right. You young people generally are. If your only interest in him is as an alliance for business purposes then it is right that you should say so.' Her lip curled. She did not sound as if she thought that anything Francesca had ever said or thought in her life was right.

The over-furnished dining room began to dance before Francesca's eyes. She teetered on her high heels and put a hand against the wall to steady herself.

'Alliance?' she croaked.

'Since we are avoiding misunderstanding, I will not hide from you,' said ex-Queen Angelika in measured tones, 'that I do not agree with my husband on this.' She flung some heavily chased forks and spoons onto the polished table in a much less measured fashion.

This is a nightmare, thought Francesca. She cleared her throat. 'What alliance?' she managed.

Her hostess was banging the cutlery into place with angry, jabbing movements.

'It may be all very modern and sensible but I think we should have some good old-fashioned affection involved. Even if you do not believe in love, you should at least like and respect each other. I do not want my Conrad to have another disaster—' She broke off in displeasure. 'Where are you going?'

'I need to speak to my father,' said Francesca grimly.

No wonder the old twister had looked so uneasy in the taxi. He must have had this up his sleeve all the time.

She forgot her uncertainty on the high heels. She was so anxious to come to grips with her father that she nearly broke into a run down the dark corridor.

'Dad—'

But even as she did so the doorbell rang. She was passing. On a simple reflex she opened it.

'Hello. The family is…'

And fell silent, blinking.

The first thing she thought was, foolishly, *Those photographs didn't show the half of it.*

The black and white portrait had caught the heavy-lidded eyes, fair enough. It had made him look sexy and remote. But this man was not remote. What the portrait had missed by a mile was the piercing quality of the gaze. When the man actually looked at you it felt as if he was stripping you. Not to the skin; to the *bone*.

And he was still horribly sexy.

'Glug,' said Francesca. Or something to that effect. She held on to the door to support her.

Vaguely, somewhere in the back of her mind, there was the sensation of total familiarity, as if she had known Prince Conrad forever. And a lot further to the forefront of her mind, blood and sinew, there was a much more basic sensation. Hunger. That damned photograph of him against the mountains had shown too many muscles, too much tanned torso. She knew exactly what was under the crisp white shirt. Within touching distance.

And those steady eyes, with that hint of laughter and their cool detachment. She knew how they looked, too. She just had never expected to have to sustain that amused regard from a distance of six inches.

She swallowed hard. Raised her eyes. And could not think of one damn thing to say.

Conrad stopped dead.

His first thought, illogical and utterly primitive, was—*Felix has read my mind!*

Well, no, actually his first thought was even more illogical and primitive than that, and involved scooping the woman under his arm and running like hell for the nearest cave. He repressed it.

He had wanted to see her so badly. Now that she was there, he knew how much. It had been eating away at him for days.

Every time he looked up from his work, every time the lab test results were late and he had to wait, every time he stood in a supermarket queue or waited for a kettle to boil—that was when her image slipped out of the shadows again. And always with the same question: *Am I a wide-eyed innocent or a calculating harridan?* And—which made him clench his jaw so hard that his teeth hurt—*Do you fancy me so much that you don't care?*

The phone number and email address which Gavron and Blake's publicity assistant had scribbled for him was dogeared. He had taken it out of his pocket so many times. And put it back again, leaving the number undialled, the email unwritten.

So far he had held out against the allure of Peter Heller's daughter. But Conrad knew that it was a close thing.

In the days since that silly party he could not count the number of times he had looked at his schedule and wondered how much time a trip to the bookshop by the gasworks would actually take. And decided that it was not a good use of his time. And kicked himself for that eminently rational decision.

Rational? Oh, sure, he was rational. Calm and in control, as always? Not by a million miles!

All the time, in his heart of hearts, he had been betting himself how much longer he was going to hang on to his principles and keep his distance from Peter Heller's daughter. Even today, he had a half-formed plan to drop into the bookshop after class. Then, once Felix demanded his presence for lunch, later in the afternoon.

And now she was here. *Here!*

But how the hell did Felix find out? And how had he kept it to himself?

All this morning, when he was persuading Conrad to talk to the old crook about a donation to the Montassurran Relief Fund, he had never once mentioned Francesca Heller. Conrad had thought of her, of course. Thought of her? Hell, he had had to fight down the wave of sheer physical longing, as if it was an incoming tidal wave.

The moment Felix said the name Peter Heller, Conrad was face to face with the enigma of his daughter. Also her troublesome habit of haunting his dreams. And her inability to decide whether, when she wandered through those dark groves, she was a witch or a fairy princess. Or was it his dilemma rather than hers?

But Felix had never said so much as her name. Certainly never hinted that she would be at this lunch. That was high-class manipulation, even by Felix's standards. What was he up to?

Well, if he thought Conrad was going to keel over and do

whatever Peter Heller wanted because he was so dazzled by his daughter Felix was very much mistaken.

Today there was no hint of the misty-eyed innocent left. In fact, her eyes were brought into sharp focus by the fashionable frames she was wearing. And she was at least two inches taller and several light-years more fashionable than she had been on that rain-washed balcony.

He felt inexplicable anger rise as he surveyed her. The soft cream and gold outfit was clearly tailored by an expert. Her hair was swept up as smoothly as a ballet dancer's. Her fingernails were expertly painted. He caught a faint, luxurious whiff of a scent that he was certain would be much too exclusive for him to recognise.

No question about it. This was no innocent bookseller. This was a clear-eyed professional woman. This was exactly the sort of woman he would have expected to find as Peter Heller's daughter. An expensive sophisticate, wholly in charge of her own life.

And he still wanted her.

Enraged at himself, Conrad rapped out, 'What are you doing here?'

Neither of the photographs had begun to catch the essence of the man. Not the athlete's build. Not how broad-shouldered he was in the flesh. How narrow-hipped. For all he was so tall, he was as lithe as a duellist. Or how he fairly sizzled with energy. Simple physical drive was like a furnace inside him.

But he was looking at her as if he hated her.

Francesca took an involuntary step back as if she had got too close to the fire. What did I *do?* she thought, bewildered. She pushed her glasses back up her nose defensively.

But she said with spirit, 'I was invited to lunch. I opened the door because I was passing. Sorry if you were expecting the butler.'

They glared at each other.

Conrad was the first to recover. 'Of course not. My grandparents have never been able to afford a butler. They're not the sort of royalty who escaped with the crown jewels.' He held out his hand. 'Conrad Domitio.'

'I guessed.' She shook it. 'Francesca Heller.'

'I know.'

He knew. He *knew*? Did that he mean he also knew all the stuff about unromantic alliances? Had he—shocking thought—already agreed? Was she the only one nobody had bothered to inform? She wanted to kill.

'Oh, really?' she began militantly.

He came in and closed the door. Without exactly pushing past her, he surged into the flat like a typhoon.

'Where is everybody? In the drawing room?'

He was polite enough now but his eyes were guarded. Guarded and watchful. So maybe he was as much in the dark as she was. Her anger subsided. And doubt took its place— doubt and a little flicker of something like recognition again.

She said abruptly, 'Have we met before?'

His eyes narrowed to chips of granite. He looked at her, unspeaking. Ice came off him in waves.

Then he said levelly, 'I don't know. You tell me. Have we?'

Surely she would have remembered those heavy-lidded eyes with their deceptive laziness and their hidden intensity? Surely she would have remembered that energy?

She said, 'I'm sorry. I don't remember.'

He gave a small nod as if it was no more than he expected.

'Then we haven't,' he said, still in that level voice.

So why didn't she believe him?

She nearly asked there and then. Nearly challenged him to justify that equivocal answer. But then the ex-king and her father came out into the hall and a more pressing matter took precedence.

'Dad,' she said, stepping into her father's path and fixing him with a glittering eye. 'Can I have a word? In private.'

He wriggled. Of course he wriggled. But the request suited ex-King Felix very well.

'Of course. Of course,' he said affably. 'Use my study. Then come and have a drink before lunch. We have some real Montassurran mead for you to try, Francesca.'

He waved them into another small dark room with, if possible, even more furniture than the rest of the apartment.

Francesca poked her father in the chest. 'What the *hell* do you think you're doing?'

Alarmed, he retreated behind a free-standing globe. 'Now, Franny, you promised you'd behave.'

'That was before I knew you were playing Napoleon,' said Francesca furiously. 'Arranged marriage, for heaven's sake! What am I, Marie Antoinette?'

'You were the one who wanted to meet the crown prince.'

'Meet, yes. But this marry! It's unreal.'

He did not say anything.

'I mean, it went out with the nineteenth century, let alone the twenty-first.'

He said, 'Are you seeing anyone at the moment?'

Francesca cast her eyes to the discoloured and peeling ceiling paper. 'You know I'm not. You just got rid of the only man in my life.'

'Pshaw. I only helped you to see the truth,' said Peter impatiently.

She could not deny it. But she did not have to like it. She folded her lips together, and said nothing.

Peter puffed. 'I don't understand women. The man was a fraud. Forget him.'

'I'm working on it,' said Francesca, glaring.

'Fine. Then today will take you further along the path to recovery.'

Her eyes narrowed to slits.

He said hastily, 'You have to be practical. One disastrous young man is not the end of the world. You just have to—'

'If you tell me to get back on the bicycle I shall leave this bloody lunch party *right now*,' said Francesca dangerously.

Peter looked at her consideringly. He decided she meant it. He tried another tack.

'I have more experience than you,' he said paternally. 'Believe me, you must not let one bad experience turn you sour. Or frighten you out of trying again. Because some people don't tell the truth it does not mean that everyone is untrustworthy.'

Francesca looked at him in outrage. Father Christmas could have taken a few tips from him, so benevolent was his demeanour.

'Very touching,' she said cynically. 'You would be more convincing if it hadn't been little more than a week since you jumped all over Barry.'

He stayed paternal. 'I know you. You are too sensitive.'

Francesca howled. *'I am not too sensitive.'*

She fairly danced with rage. And fell off her high heels.

Her father came out from behind the globe and helped her regain her balance. To her surprise, he held on to her hand.

'You dealt yourself out of the dating game a long time ago,' he said soberly. 'That Barry was your first boyfriend for— well, we will not say how long. And he was not worth it. I am so afraid that he is one disaster too many. And it's all my fault.'

She was startled. And rather touched. She shook her head. 'Of course it isn't your fault,' she said crisply. 'I'm over twenty-one. If I mess up, it's my responsibility.'

He gave a deep sigh. 'But these—' he used a Montassurran word. It sounded as if he were spitting '—fortune hunters would not be after you if it were not for my money.'

'You shouldn't have been so successful,' she teased. But she could not deny it.

He shook his head. 'I thought I was doing the right thing,' he said almost to himself. 'Working hard. Providing for my family. And where has it got me? A divorce and a daughter who can't call her private life her own.'

'It's not as bad as that,' said Francesca, startled.

'Yes, it is. Your mother told me all about it.'

She looked away, suddenly uncomfortable. 'Well, you know Mother—she thought I was on the shelf when I wasn't engaged at eighteen.'

'She would not care if you had a career you loved. But she said that before you set up that bookshop with your friend you kept losing jobs because of the reporters.'

'Well—yes.'

'How many?'

Francesca withdrew her fingers. 'Counting the receptionist's job at Harper's that I was no good at, I think I averaged about eight weeks per job,' she said lightly.

Her father looked taken aback. 'That's terrible.'

'Oh, I don't know. I learned a little about an awful lot of things. And it was better than being a full-time rich girl.'

He pounded his hand into the other palm. 'The trouble is, you're neither fish nor fowl.'

'Thank you,' said Francesca drily.

'If we had been rich all your life I would have taught you how to deal with it. You would be happy now. You wouldn't care about a job. And you would know how to deal with fortune hunters and gossip columnists.'

'Want a bet?'

He ignored that. 'And if you weren't a rich girl now you wouldn't have all these difficulties.'

'If I weren't a rich girl now I wouldn't have a lovely flat on the river and a wardrobe from Paris,' said Francesca astringently. 'Don't get carried away.'

Her father looked at her, remorseful. 'But you don't want a wardrobe from Paris. You want a husband and children.'

To her horror, Francesca felt her stomach lurch sickeningly. Even her mother had not been as blunt as that.

'Dad—'

'I've spoiled that for you. Nice men don't come near you because you're my daughter.'

Francesca said sharply, 'Who told you nice men don't come near me? That was Mother again, wasn't it?'

He did not deny it.

'Look, Dad, all right, this last couple of years has been a bit fraught. But now I've gone into partnership with Jazz, I'm fine. The shop was a bit rocky when I first went in. But now

I've started the internet book club—and the writers' readings in the evening—it's coming along just fine. It's a great life. I've found something I'm good at. I'm going to follow in your footsteps and be a career woman.'

There was a pause.

Then her father said heavily, 'Don't lie to me. You are not happy.'

She was too honest to deny it. 'Nobody gets everything they want. And believe me, there's nothing an instant engagement could do except make it worse. Even if he's the most eligible guy in the world.'

He took her hand again. 'Francesca, let me do this one thing for you. Your mother says—'

'If my mother says I need you to buy me a husband she's out of her tree,' she flashed.

He looked hurt. More than hurt. Stricken.

Francesca's conscience kicked her. 'Oh, hell, I didn't mean that.'

His shoulders sagged. He looked like a troglodyte who had just been told that he was too ugly to live in the world of men. Only a monster would have turned her back on him.

'Oh, all right,' said Francesca irritably. 'I won't walk out before lunch. But I'm not going along with this lunacy any further than that. Got it?'

'Got it,' agreed Peter Heller. 'Thank you.'

They went back into the drawing room.

The ex-king stopped talking abruptly. He and his grandson looked round. Conrad's expression was implacable and the ex-king looked worried.

'Conrad, let me introduce you properly. Peter Heller, who is being so good as to make a substantial donation to the Montassurran Hospitals Fund.'

The two men nodded guardedly. 'Well, don't forget we still have to talk about that, Felix,' said Conrad, smiling like a dagger.

'And his daughter, Francesca.'

'Francesca,' said Conrad, as if he were tasting it.

He seemed to make up his mind. The dagger smile disappeared. Along with it went all other signs of hostility. The look he gave her was—there was no other word for it—soulful. He gave her a warm smile, deep into her eyes, and came very close.

'My grandson, Crown Prince Conrad,' said the ex-king. He sounded anxious.

Does he know? thought Francesca. Was he brought here in the dark, just as I was? And has King Frog broken it to him yet? Or did he sign up to an arranged marriage right from the start?

She stared and stared but the smiling eyes were quite unreadable. For all the signs of awareness he gave, he could still be under the impression that the Hellers were there to talk about nothing but donations to the Hospitals Fund. She nearly asked him. She was on the point of asking him but...

Well, he took her hand. And all coherent thought sort of stopped.

Crown Prince Conrad appeared to be debating internally. In fact, he looked, thought Francesca, more shaken than she wanted to admit, as if for two pennies he would go into a full Imperial Guard bow and kiss her fingertips.

She didn't know whether he thought that would make her keener to marry him or put her off terminally. She didn't care. She was quite sure Crown Prince Conrad thought it would embarrass her. And would enjoy doing it for that reason alone. She glared.

'Well? Have we met before?' she said challengingly.

Conrad gave her his most beguiling smile. 'How foolish of me. Of course not. How could I have forgotten? Forgive me.'

'Forget it,' said Francesca brusquely, unbeguiled.

She retrieved her hand.

There was one of those sharp silences, where you could almost read the thought balloons above people's heads. Felix looked uneasy, Peter Heller downright affronted. While Francesca, as she saw from an unfortunately placed hall mirror, looked as sullen as a schoolgirl, for all her Paris elegance.

Well, at least she did not look as if she were trying to attract the man, she thought, trying to comfort herself.

Conrad, alone of the company, seemed to be amused by it. He grinned.

'What about a drink, Grandad? If you're giving Mr Heller the full guide to Montassurran culture I assume you've broken out the mead?'

'Not yet. I was waiting for you.' And waved him to the drinks tray.

Peter Heller greeted the subject with relief.

'My grandmother used to make mead,' he said with an effortful chattiness that made Francesca want to scream. 'She used to call it quadruple. And put chilli pepper in. Or did I imagine that?'

'Capsicumel,' said his hostess, returning to the drawing room. 'Good afternoon, Conrad.' She did not wait for an answer. 'But how advanced, Mr Heller. Your grandmother must have been a real experimenter. But quadruple refers to the proportion of honey used. We drink quadruple here, but usually only as an after-dinner digestif. It is very strong.'

'And very sweet,' said Conrad. He was dealing with bottles and glasses at the drinks tray on the bureau but now he looked round, dark eyes gleaming with laughter. 'Rots your teeth as well as making your head spin.'

'Oh, a real bonus,' muttered Francesca.

Her father winced.

'Do you drink it at home, Mr Heller?' asked the ex-queen quickly.

'No. I haven't had medu since I left Montassurro. Of course, I never thought to take any of the old recipes with me. I was only fourteen. I wasn't thinking about traditions. I was thinking about the Ferrari I was going to get one day.' He laughed.

So did the others, although to Francesca it seemed their laughter was hollow.

'And how many Ferraris do you own now?' asked Conrad, with deceptive innocence.

At least, Francesca knew it was deceptive. Peter Heller just shook his head and answered factually.

'By the time I was rich enough to run one, all I wanted from a car was a smooth ride while someone else did the driving. These days I just sit in the back and talk on the phone.'

'Oh, the penalties of wealth,' mourned Conrad.

Francesca sent him a furious look. But he was debating among some fearsome stone bottles and did not see. His grandfather did, though. He leaped into the breach.

'So it took some time to build, this empire of yours?'

Peter nodded. He was always comfortable when he talked about his business.

'For a long time there was no empire,' he said ruefully. 'I lived all over the world, trading a bit of this, a bit of that. Learning all the time, of course. Then my financial advisers made a mess of my portfolio. And I thought—I can do better than that. Never looked back. But it was only...what would you say, Francesca...six years ago?'

'Seven and a half,' said Francesca without emphasis.

'Oh, that accuracy of yours,' said her father, torn between irritation and amusement. He said to the others, 'She should have been an accountant. She is so precise.'

Francesca shrugged. 'I have a good memory,' she said, almost at random.

Of course, she had good reason to remember the date her father had gone global. She had been nearly sixteen, good at languages, going to be a teacher. And then suddenly she was an international jet setter, good at nothing, not staying in any school more than a few weeks, with a mother who was determined to make her a social success, and no viable future at all except spending her father's money. She knew to the day when Peter Heller had made it into New York's richest one hundred.

The prince brought over a small tray, exquisitely inlaid, with two glasses on it. As he passed her chair there was a faint, aromatic stir of the air. Pine and wood smoke. Francesca froze.

She hardly noticed as the ex-king debated, then chose a glass and handed it to Peter.

'Try this. See if it reminds you.'

Peter Heller tasted in silence for a moment. Then he said, 'Apples. That's cyser, isn't it? How well I remember.'

His host and hostess looked relieved. They began a rather laboured discussion of methods of brewing mead practised in Montassurro in the ex-king's youth.

Francesca did not even try to take an interest. She was too conscious of Prince Conrad.

If it had not been crazy she would have said...

But of course it was crazy. The trouble was that she had not been able to get the guy from the balcony out of her mind. She knew the reasons, too. Rebound and delayed adolescence. She reminded herself of them every day. That had to be the reason she was sensing him here among her father's cronies.

But Prince Conrad had been at that publisher's party.

Yes, but the balcony man was someone quite different. She had even asked him if he knew Prince Conrad and he'd said he didn't. Well, she thought he'd said he didn't. She frowned, trying to remember.

A glass appeared in front of her suddenly. She looked up, startled.

'Try this,' said Conrad, his dark face wickedly amiable. 'I'm betting this is the one for you. Didn't think you'd like apples. See if I've guessed right.'

Francesca sipped. Very, very cautiously.

She was glad to concentrate on the odd taste.

'Is it really honey? Really? It doesn't taste like it.'

She sipped again. It did not taste anything like as sugary as she expected. In fact, it tasted of *perfume*. She said so.

To her surprise, Conrad looked pleased. Genuinely pleased this time, not that horrible teasing pretence.

'Rhodomel. Mixed with attar of roses. Do you like it?'

Francesca went back to the drink. 'I don't know. What's attar of thingy?'

'A distillate of rose petals. Very rare. Very precious.' He

paused deliberately. 'Legend says it was made originally for the sultan's favourite, so that she could hold his love forever.'

'Oh?'

There was no reason that she could think of that the information should make her blush. Francesca met his dancing eyes for a pregnant moment. He smiled and sat down beside her on the sofa.

'And of course it's always been supposed to turn mead into an aphrodisiac,' he murmured.

In the act of taking a longer swallow, Francesca choked. Rose-petal distillate was sucked into her airway. She began to cough helplessly.

Conrad gave her a helpful thump between the shoulder blades.

'Don't worry. I'm used to it. I'll calm you down if you get frisky.'

'That won't be necessary,' said Francesca, though she could barely speak. Her throat felt as if it was on fire.

'Conrad, pour Miss Heller a glass of water,' instructed his grandmother, noticing at last. 'We forget how powerful medu can be for people who aren't used to it.'

'Not Miss Heller,' said Conrad wickedly, though he got up and brought her water. 'She's immune.' He gave it to her. 'Isn't that right?'

Her father looked bewildered. 'Francesca isn't much of a drinker.'

She put the rose-scented poison down on a fussily decorated table with a decisive smack.

'Oh, not there, dear,' said her hostess, leaping up to field it. 'The veneer is so delicate.'

'Sorry,' said Francesca. Still fighting for breath, she did not sound it.

There was another tingling silence.

Conrad looked down at her. Francesca was certain that he was thoroughly enjoying himself. He looked so confident, so in control. As if he knew what was going on and she didn't.

There was another little kick of memory. Oh, God, that

balcony guy had really done a number on her. She was seeing him everywhere!

Conrad gave a slow smile. *Because he thinks I want to get engaged to him? Or because he's damn certain I don't?* wondered Francesca. It was, she thought, going to be a long, long lunch. But at least it couldn't get any worse.

In that she was wrong.

Well, not wholly wrong. The food was delicious. Once they were seated, the conversation even picked up a bit. She had hardly ever heard her father talk about his homeland and it was intriguing. If only she had not had the terrible feeling that her hosts were being offered the chance to look her over as part of a package deal she would almost have enjoyed herself.

Crown Prince Conrad did not take much part, of course. In fact, Crown Prince Conrad spent most of the time looking as if he were watching a comedy on prime-time television. But if Francesca kept her eyes on her hosts or the tablecloth she did not have to fight the almost irresistible urge to hit him.

The meal drew to an excruciating close. Francesca's contribution to the conversation went from monosyllables to silence. Across the table Crown Prince Conrad sparkled wittily, giving her yet another reason, if she wanted it, to hate him.

Let me get out without disgracing myself, she prayed.

She nearly managed it. So nearly.

And then she overheard him...

Well, her mother had always said that eavesdroppers never heard any good of themselves. But Francesca had never intended to be an eavesdropper. It was the last thing in the world she wanted. Only the overcrowded flat was deceptive and on her way back from the bathroom she turned through the wrong door and found herself at one end of an L-shaped kitchen.

At the other end, out of sight round the corner, two people were talking. A man with a velvet, dark voice that was somehow familiar. More than familiar. So familiar that she almost went round the corner to see who he was.

And then she realised that they were arguing, from the tone of their voices. Francesca had grown up very sensitive to tone.

She knew this was an argument before she heard the words. Before she even realised who was speaking.

Embarrassed, she was turning to make good her escape before they knew anyone had overheard them, when a single sentence arrested her.

'She was my guest and you were rude.' So that identified the woman. Ex-queen Angelika, clearly. She sounded upset. Angry, even. 'You haven't given her a chance.'

'A *chance*? Am I interviewing her for a job here?'

'Be sensible, Conrad.'

Oh, so that was whose the other voice was. Francesca was surprised. She had not realised how deep his voice was when he was mocking her with aphrodisiac rose petals and a superabundance of Ferraris.

Again, memory stirred. *Surely* she knew that voice? And she didn't associate it with sarcastic Crown Prince Conrad, either.

It made him seem more substantial somehow. Someone to be reckoned with. A man of substance rather than the mocking trickster who had teased her all through this horrible lunch party.

Her hand on the door knob, Francesca hesitated. She knew it was wrong to listen without telling them she was there. But he sounded so different that Francesca was taken aback.

'Grandmama, I *am* sensible,' he said crisply. 'I spend my whole life being sensible. I do my job, pay my taxes, support my community. And that's *it*.' There was the sound of a hand smacking down on a table. Francesca heard glassware ring. 'I'm not into human sacrifice.'

'But your grandfather thinks that—'

'My grandfather thinks that he's Napoleon,' said Conrad coldly. Francesca nearly applauded: great minds did indeed think alike! 'Well, he's not making political alliances with my private life.'

Francesca's hand froze to the door knob. She found she was shaking.

Well, there was the answer to the conundrum. Conrad

Domitio knew what was being planned all right. And had been sitting there all through lunch, trying to avoid it. So he must have thought she had agreed, signed up—and come here specifically to try to attract him!

From ice, she went to white-hot. White-hot rage. White-hot embarrassment. She did not know which was stronger.

Ex-Queen Angelika sounded a lot more human than Francesca would ever have believed. 'He's only trying to do what's best.'

The dark velvet voice gentled. 'I know he is, Grandmama. But he can't do it by making everyone dance to his tune. And this idea of marriage is just—unrealistic.'

'Oh, my dear.' It sounded as if she was going to cry. 'Still Silvia?'

'Aaaaagh!' This time it was not only the glassware. Crockery and baking tins rattled as well. 'This has nothing to do with whether I might or might not want to marry again at some time in the future.' The dark voice wasn't velvet any more. It was steel and it rasped with exasperation. 'Let's get this clear. I am never going to marry Francesca Heller. Never. *I'm* too poor. *She's* too plain. And she's much, much too prickly. Got it?'

CHAPTER FOUR

CONRAD'S head shot up. 'What was that noise?'

Though, of course, to one who had spent his morning teaching against a background of students sneaking into class late, it was unmistakeable. Someone had just eased a door shut. Someone who did not want to draw attention to the fact that the door had ever opened in the first place. But which door?

Then he remembered. His grandmother's kitchen was L-shaped! Somebody could have been out of sight in the other arm of the room. Somebody could have been standing there a long time. Somebody could have heard every single word!

'What noise?' said his grandmother, seeing the change in his face.

'Someone was listening…'

He strode round the corner, into other arm of the kitchen. It was empty. Well, of course it was. He would not have heard the door close so gently if the listener had still been there. Whoever it was, he or she had wanted to slip out undetected.

Conrad did not have to think too hard to work out why. He groaned.

'There's no one here,' said his grandmother, following. She looked bewildered.

'Of course not. She heard what I said and bolted.'

'Who did?'

'You don't want to know.'

'Don't be silly. Of course I do.'

'Well, if you really want an answer, I'd put money on the woman I've just been calling plain and prickly,' said Conrad with a grim smile.

His grandmother pressed both hands to her face in the age-old gesture of dismay. *'No!'*

'I told you that you didn't want to know.'

'But what on earth was she doing in here?'

He shrugged.

'Maybe Marta got back early,' said his grandmother, determined to look on the bright side.

'Sorry, Grandmama. No loud music, no coffee brewing. Ergo no Marta. You know it as well as I do. No, it must have been Francesca Heller.'

'What can we do?' said the ex-queen, frowning. 'Your grandfather was really counting on Peter Heller.'

Conrad gave a snort of laughter. 'Grandmama, you're all heart. I've just comprehensively insulted the woman and all you care about is her father?'

His grandmother shrugged. 'She shouldn't have been listening to a private conversation.'

'You don't like her, do you?' said Conrad, slowly.

'Nor do you. I've never heard you call a woman plain and prickly before.'

'She got me on the raw. But I shouldn't have lost my temper.'

His grandmother was thoughtful. 'Yes, she did, didn't she?'

But Conrad was pursuing his own line of thought. 'I should never have said it.' He was really disturbed. 'I'll have to apologise.'

'You can't,' said his grandmother practically. 'You didn't say it to her. She was eavesdropping. She may not want to admit that.' She sniffed. 'A decently brought-up girl wouldn't! Anyway, you can't apologise for thinking something. Especially if it's true.'

The heavy-lidded eyes lifted. 'True?'

'Well, she is plain.'

'Do you think so?'

'Of course. She ought to pluck her eyebrows. And those terrible glasses! That hair! No one would think she had all that money to spend on hairdressers!'

'I suppose so,' said Conrad. He sounded constrained.

'Squat, too,' said his grandmother with relish. 'She must be used to people calling her plain.'

'Not me, though.'

'I wouldn't worry,' said his grandmother shrewdly. 'Your image won't have taken too much of a blow. I don't think she was exactly falling in love with you, even before you trashed her.'

He could not really challenge that. Though for some reason it irritated him deeply.

'Damn!' He strode restlessly about the kitchen. 'I never meant to hurt the woman's feelings.'

'That only makes it worse,' said his grandmother.

Conrad narrowed his eyes at her. 'You sound almost gleeful about it.'

She chuckled. 'Well, you were so positive that you were in control of everything. It's nice to see you can be tripped up, just like the rest of us.'

'It's beginning to be a habit with Francesca Heller,' he said ironically.

His grandmother was startled. 'What? When? How?'

Conrad ignored the questions. He smote one fist into the other hand in frustration.

'I have to do something!'

'You can't,' said his grandmother with malicious satisfaction. 'You'll have to pretend that you didn't say it. And she'll have to pretend she didn't hear it. You'll both do fine.'

'Oh, great! That's really going to make the party go with a swing.'

His grandmother relented. 'They'll be going home soon. After that, you need never see her again.'

Conrad did not find that a consolation. His irritation increased. He did not make much attempt to hide it.

His grandmother bit back a smile and let him carry the coffee into the drawing room.

She was right. The visitors did not prolong their stay. In fact, Francesca virtually flung her coffee down her throat and stood up in one single movement. Her father observed it with foreboding.

'We ought to make a move,' she said firmly.

He looked at his boiling-hot coffee and the glass of liqueur-strength mead that stood untested at his elbow. 'Surely, there's plenty of time,' he protested.

For what? thought Francesca, on the edge of hysteria.

'I promised Jazz I would get back to the shop this afternoon,' she said, artificially calm and not at all truthful.

'But I told you we would be going out for the whole day.'

Peter Heller did not like to be crossed and usually wasn't. He had half expected Francesca to refuse to come at all. When she agreed to the lunch party—at last—he had not anticipated further rebellion. Now he saw that he had misjudged his daughter.

'Saturday is our busy day,' she announced. That *was* true. She gave her hostess a blinding smile. 'I'm sure you understand.'

The ex-queen had never worked in a shop in her life but she said warmly, 'Of course, dear.' And meant it.

She was going to get out of here in relatively good order, thought Francesca, though she was shaking with temper. And something more than temper.

It was one thing for her mother to tell her that she was too dull to attract any man who had an alternative. It was quite another to overhear a complete stranger say she was plain and prickly.

Prickly! She'd show him prickly.

If she ever saw him again. Which, of course, she wouldn't. Not if she could help it. And she could. She was never going to let her father blackmail her into anything like this ever again. Nor dashing Prince Conrad either.

When he shook hands with her as they prepared to leave she virtually tore her hand out of his grasp.

He looked taken aback—then suddenly serious. Probably seeing a fortune walking out of the door, thought Francesca with savage satisfaction.

He leaned towards her. 'Look, can we talk? Privately, I mean,' he murmured.

'No.'

He blinked. Obviously shattered that anyone could resist him, thought Francesca. After all the pseudo-polite needling at lunch, he suddenly realised he had to *try*. Well, too late, buster.

He was not deterred. 'This lunch party was not a good idea,' he admitted, still in that confidential tone. 'But there are things I'd like to—er—discuss.'

Francesca froze. For a moment she thought wildly that this was where everyone expected him to ask her for a date. And Crown Prince Conrad wanted to explain that it was not going to happen. Would he tell her she was plain and prickly to her face? She found she was shaking.

Indignation, she assured herself. Totally justified indignation. She looked across to where Peter was taking fulsome leave of the ex-queen.

'Oh, I think it's all pretty clear,' she said ironically. 'No explanation necessary.'

'But there is.' He sounded urgent suddenly. 'I was annoyed at—well, we can talk about that later. I felt my grandfather had been jerking my strings. But that was no reason for—er—being insulting about you.'

Francesca looked at him in outrage. 'Are you apologising to me?'

'Yes—no.' He pushed a hand through the springy hair. *'Hell!'*

'Quite.' She turned away. 'Hell just about covers it.'

He stepped in front of her. 'Look, I'm sorry, right?'

He sounded impatient. Well, at least he wasn't patronising her any more.

'That makes two of us.'

He considered her for a fraught moment. Then, 'You aren't very forgiving, are you?' he said ruefully.

Francesca gave him a wide, furious smile. If Peter and the

royalty were watching they would think she and the Crown Prince were enjoying a joke in best social style.

'I'm my father's daughter. We're great grudge-holders.'

'So I see.' A note of unholy amusement invaded the deep voice. 'And I am sorry. Really. I never meant to hurt your feelings... Can't we meet somewhere?'

'You didn't hurt my feelings,' she said curtly. 'I imagine you look down your nose at everybody. I don't take it personally. And no, we can't.'

Look down my nose...?

He was thunderstruck. Francesca began to enjoy herself for the first time that day.

'I thought it was a bit old-fashioned, to be honest,' she said airily. 'I mean, this day and age! People don't take all that divine right of kings seriously any more, do they?' And added, a lot less innocently, 'Especially when the kings in question are a bunch of mountain brigands.'

His reaction to that surprised her. She expected anger. Indignation. Even that flash of fury in the hooded eyes, perhaps. She looked forward to that.

But what she got was a steady stare. And, under the cover of Peter's appreciative farewells, an unnerving silence.

Then he drawled, 'Do you get a lot of entertainment out of that one?'

'What?'

'The Domitio family as Montassurro's answer to *The Godfather*,' he explained blandly.

Francesca puffed. 'Are you saying it's not true?'

'You know it isn't.'

She fired up. 'My father always says—'

'Your father,' he said deliberately, 'is in no position to talk about brigands.'

Their eyes met with a clash like swords.

Francesca drew in a hissing breath. 'I don't see you turning down his money.'

He was amused. 'That's no argument. And you know it.'

She did, too. She knew quite well that her father's donation was going to fund a mobile hospital unit in Montassurro. Of course Conrad Domitio was not going to turn that down, no matter what he thought of Peter Heller's business ethics.

She was nearly choking with anger. 'The Domitio family may not be mafia. But you've always been great exploiters, haven't you?'

'What?'

'I looked you up on the internet,' she said with satisfaction.

His eyes narrowed to black slits of contempt.

'Do you always check the web gossip on your hosts?' It bit.

If Francesca had been less angry—or less hurt—she would have backed down then. She didn't.

'I like to be briefed when I'm meeting strangers.' And then added bitterly, fatally, 'So many people who look respectable turn out to be con men.'

She was thinking of Barry de la Touche when she said it. Or Barry Trott, as she now knew him to be. But, of course, Prince Conrad did not know that.

She only realised that she had gone too far when she saw a muscle in his cheek begin to throb.

He said over his shoulder, 'You ought to show Miss Heller the family tree, Felix. She thinks you're a con artist.'

His lips barely moved but his voice soared. If he had been calling to a distant mountaintop, like one of his swashbuckling ancestors, his voice could not have carried more clearly. Or been more devastating.

That was when she realised just how far her indignation had taken her.

'No,' said Francesca, appalled.

The older men swung round, shocked. The ex-queen retreated to a window-seat.

'Francesca!' bellowed her father.

The ex-king lost his courteous smile at last. 'Miss Heller thinks *what?*'

She was engulfed by wretched heat. She could feel it in her cheeks. 'I never meant—'

Now she was the one on the wrong foot, floundering and apologising, while this family of snobs looked down their aquiline noses at her.

Oh, he had turned the tables on her, all right. First he called her plain and prickly. Then he flung her to the wolves. Francesca glared at Prince Conrad with real hatred.

The ex-queen watched thoughtfully.

'The line of descent is very clear,' said the ex-king arctically. 'No one has ever doubted it. Not even the communists. Not even the *anarchists*. They might not have wanted a king. But they did not doubt that the Domitio family had the right.' The look he sent Francesca classed her a long way below either communists or anarchists.

'Prince Conrad misunderstood,' she said between gritted teeth.

Prince Conrad looked down at her with totally spurious concern. 'Oh?' he queried mildly. 'How? You said that people often turned out to be con men.'

'Yes, I know,' she said, hating him. 'But I was speaking generally. Not specifically. Not about—'

'Me?' It was silkily said. And an unmistakeable challenge. Francesca felt the hairs on the back of her neck rise, as if she were an animal scenting danger.

'Anyone here,' she said desperately.

She looked at her father in supplication. But there was no help coming from that quarter. He was looking stunned.

And then the ex-queen said quietly, 'Francesca has a point.'

All eyes turned to her, in varying degrees of astonishment and affront. She smiled.

'Not about the family tree, perhaps. But about not taking people on trust. I think that is very sensible. You and I would have done better if we had been a little more cautious about people, Felix.'

It was Peter's turn to stiffen, scenting an insult. Conrad bit back a smile and turned away.

Not quickly enough. Francesca saw it. She decided hate was too good for him.

Defeat, that was what Prince Conrad Domitio needed. Total, public defeat. She wanted to wipe that superior smile off his face. Force him into a humiliating climb-down. For a moment she had a hot fantasy in which he acknowledged that her father was his equal; that a woman was justified in being wary about obscure ex-royalty; that his grandfather was a bore, his grandmother too sugary to live; that Montassurran mead was undrinkable; and that Francesca was neither plain *nor* prickly.

Oh, she wanted supercilious Prince Conrad to *grovel*.

This pleasant picture flickered and died as the ex-king gave a long sigh. He said ruefully, 'You are right, of course, my dear. These young people are so much more worldly than we were.'

From the look he spared Francesca, it was not intended as a compliment.

'So perhaps Miss Heller would like to see a little of the old ways,' said the ex-queen smoothly. 'The Montassurran community has a party every year on Black Conrad's birthday. This year the proceeds go to the Hospitals Appeal. We would be so pleased if you would come as our guest, my dear.'

The strained silence that greeted this announcement was a clear indication that she lied in her teeth, thought Francesca. Ex-King Felix would not be pleased at all. And Prince Conrad looked positively horrified.

That was what made up her mind. Him grovelling would be better. But grovelling would have to wait. For the moment she would settle for his horrified acquiescence.

'How kind of you,' she said pleasurably.

Conrad curbed his fury with visible effort. Francesca's smile widened.

'I shall look forward to it,' she assured them.

After that, they were glad enough to let her go. Even her father did not send more than one wistful half-glance at his full coffee-cup. And ex-King Felix was positively dancing with impatience to have her out of the apartment.

'I'll come down and find you a cab,' said Conrad.

Francesca stalked ahead, as if she had not heard him.

Conrad caught up with her on the pavement. He put a hand on her arm.

Once again she had a strange flash of recognition. She turned her head—and scented woodland and a wild, untamed landscape. It had to be those damned photographs, especially that one on the mountain with his kit falling off.

She gritted her teeth and banished the image.

'We've really got to talk. On neutral territory,' he muttered in her ear.

'No territory would be neutral enough,' she flashed.

A taxi cruised past, its light on. Peter raised his umbrella and darted to the kerb.

'It'll have to be,' said Conrad. 'I'll call you.'

'No, you won't.' Francesca was thoroughly roused, way beyond any consideration of good manners or even her own dignity. She swung round on him, so infuriated that she was perfectly steady in spite of her spindle heels. 'I don't ever want to see you again.'

The taxi cruised to a stop and her father bent to talk to the driver.

'You should have thought of that before you accepted my grandmother's invitation to the ball.'

She had forgotten that. She bit her lip. Then shrugged, recovering. 'I can get out of it if I want. A headache. A bout of food poisoning. I'll manufacture something suitable.'

'You sound as if you've had years of practice at dodging social engagements.'

'I have.'

'Coward,' he said softly.

She flushed, not looking at him. 'All right, then. I'll just say I changed my mind.'

He laughed. 'You don't know my grandmother. You signed up. Now there's no way you'll get out of it short of having a contagious disease. Though I suppose emigration's a possibility.'

She was so angry she could have cried. His teasing laughter was like a slap in the face.

'No one can make me go to a stupid party,' she hissed. 'I'm an independent woman. No one can make me do anything I don't want to.'

'Want a bet?'

Quick as a snake, she rounded on him. 'Don't confuse me with the bunch of hangers-on you're clearly used to.'

He blinked. 'Hangers-on? What are you talking about?'

'Some people may be willing to turn backward somersaults just so they get to play kings and queens,' raged Francesca in a strangled under-voice. 'I'm not one of them. Get lost.'

She almost pushed her father out of the way and dived into the taxi.

'What an awful woman. I'm sorry, Conrad,' said his grandfather.

The two men were propped against the kitchen cabinets while the ex-queen loaded the dishwasher. They were forbidden on pain of death to help, though Conrad had been permitted to decant leftovers and put them in the fridge. The Domitios' elderly maid, when she returned from taking her grandson to the football match, would patrol the kitchen and present a report on her employers' failures in the care and cleanliness department.

'Well, I wasn't very nice to her,' Conrad said uncomfortably to the back of his grandmother's head.

'I should think not. I've never met a girl with less charm.' Ex-King Felix waved his cigar, to the imminent danger of several cooking implements hanging on the wall. 'I doubt if Casanova himself could have got a smile out of her.' He turned remorseful eyes on Conrad. 'Forget her father's money. He'll cough up for the Hospitals Fund, now that he's promised. But we won't ask him for any more donations.'

'Well, that's a good thing, at least,' said Conrad. He made an effort to concentrate on his grandfather's affairs. 'Other donations? Donations to what?'

Felix looked cunning. 'I have an idea about the elections.'

'Elections?' Conrad was blank.

'In Montassurro. They have asked me to stand for president. On a non-political ticket, of course,' he said sunnily.

'What?'

'So I'm starting a campaign fund.'

Conrad straightened. 'Not with Peter Heller's money,' he said grimly.

'No,' agreed his grandfather, losing some of his sparkle. 'Though it would have come in useful. But there, I should have known there was something wrong with the girl when he suggested it. At least I should have met her first. If I had I would never have tried to get you two together. That girl bites.'

Conrad ignored most of this. 'He suggested it?' he said in an odd voice.

'Yes. We were having lunch and he got a phone call from her. After that he said…' Felix broke off. 'What is it?' he said, alarmed.

For Conrad, calm, logical, cool-headed Conrad, was clenching his fists as if he wanted to hit someone.

He said in a level voice his grandfather had never heard from him before, 'Let me get this clear. Francesca Heller put her father up to putting in a bid for my hand in marriage?'

His grandmother raised her eyebrows.

Felix said, 'Well, I gather some chap just…' he waved a hand, embarrassed.

'Dumped her?' suggested Conrad, still level.

'I suppose that's what you'd call it. Yes.'

'So I'm the consolation prize?'

'Now, Conrad—'

'And she picked it out herself! What Francesca wants, Francesca gets.'

'Hussy,' said Felix, bewildered but sympathising.

Conrad ignored him. 'Daddy's going to buy me for her.'

'The heir to the Montassurran tradition is not for sale,' said Felix grandly. 'Not for all the donations in the world.'

The ex-queen snapped the dishwasher shut with rather more violence than was required.

'Oh, stop wittering, Felix. Her father's donations have nothing to do with it. Conrad will judge for himself, exactly as he always does.'

Conrad came out of his uncharacteristic fury. The muscle still jumped in his jaw. It seemed he could not control it. But, when he spoke, it was in his habitual drawl. 'Yes, I will.'

His grandparents exchanged glances. They knew that look. It did not bode well for Francesca Heller.

'So there's no need for you to see the girl again, right?' said Felix nervously.

Conrad smiled. It was a slow, slow smile and it did not reach his eyes at all.

'Oh, but there is,' he said.

It was gentle.

And deadly.

He was still in the grip of icy rage when he turned the car into the traffic and headed for the motorway.

OK, he should not have called her plain and prickly. He should not have let her overhear him either. He should have challenged her the moment he walked in. Not allowed her to pretend they had never met before. He should have called her as big a con artist as her father. And he should have done it to her face.

He whipped the big Range Rover through streets crowded with Saturday-afternoon shoppers. He was driving with vicious precision. He went past a street market in its last throes. Paper litter blew along the wet road surface like oversized confetti. Conrad set his teeth and resisted the temptation to drive over the inflated bags just to hear them explode. He was too mature for that sort of boy's trick.

But he wanted to. Oh, how he wanted to.

He never normally drove this road at this hour. After the morning's teaching, he usually spent time with friends. More often than not he went on to spend the evening with a girlfriend. But ever since he met Francesca Heller he had been oddly reluctant to call any of the clever, independent, sophisticated women in his address book.

For some reason that made him even more furious. Oh, what the hell? he thought—and deliberately set the car at a billowing plastic carrier bag. As he drove over it the crack was like a gunshot. Conrad laughed aloud.

That's what Francesca Heller needs, he thought. A shock. Any shock. A good, loud paper-bag explosion should shake her up. Make her question that assurance that she could make the whole damned world dance to her tune.

He dwelled savagely on the prospect of shaking up Francesca Heller. It lasted him all the way to Cambridge.

'Well?' said Jazz. 'Did you get him?'

Francesca glared. 'If you mean Crown Prince Conrad, I wouldn't touch him with a bargepole.' She dislodged a Saturday girl from the 'Enquiries' table and banged her glasses up her nose. 'Next.'

The customer so addressed jumped nervously and stammered out his question. Francesca answered without recourse to research. It was a routine query about a fashionable book and there was no great skill in it. But he backed away from the table as if he had come across fully operational supernatural power.

'Thank you. Call again,' said Francesca with a terrifying display of teeth that was meant to be a smile.

Jazz decided it was time to take action. 'Come along. Before you scare a customer into a heart attack.'

She abandoned the till to the Saturday girl and marched Francesca to the small staff cloakroom. 'Now, what the hell happened?'

Francesca turned hot eyes on her. Ever since she had left her father at his London apartment she had done nothing but pick over the horrible lunch party. She could now recite every single bit of barbed conversation in all its awfulness.

Half the time she wanted to die. The other half, she wanted

to kill. Preferably nasty, teasing, superior, dismissive, *gorgeous* Prince Conrad.

She said flatly, 'I'm plain and prickly and he doesn't want to marry me.'

'*What?*'

'My father, on the other hand, seems to have done a deal to make him do just that.'

Jazz's reaction was all she could ask. She stared, blinked, then threw her hands up in the air.

'Are all Montassurrans mad?'

'You'd think so, wouldn't you?' agreed Francesca with gloomy satisfaction.

'I asked you to invite him to a book discussion. Not *bed*.'

Francesca was indignant. 'Hey, don't take it out on me because my father's a lunatic. Anyway, the rest of the bloody family are worse.'

Jazz waved her hands around. She looked exasperated. 'How many times have I told you? Keep focus. Don't mix business with pleasure.'

'Pleasure!'

'You were supposed to be playing the network to bring the man into The Buzz. Not starting a blood feud.' She puffed out a great sigh of irritation. 'I suppose there's not a hope he'd ever darken our doors after this?'

Francesca had become quite calm suddenly. 'I've no idea. But if you want me to go on running the literary evenings, keep the man away from me. With boat hooks if necessary.'

Jazz forgot her irritation. 'Ah!'

So she was not entirely surprised when Conrad Domitio walked into The Buzz the moment they opened on Monday morning.

She was alone at the desk. The door banged back and a blast of spring air set the bookmarks fluttering. Jazz looked up—and knew who it was at once. Of course, the portrait photograph didn't show his height. But everything else was there: heavy-lidded eyes, cheekbones Dracula would have envied, sculpted, sensual mouth. And enough energy to set the world on fire.

'Where is she?' he said without preamble.

Even in the crowded bookshop, he moved as if he was striding across a wilderness: long, smooth strides; total physical co-ordination; total power.

Jazz began to smile. 'Your picture doesn't do you justice,' she told him. 'Hi, I'm Jazz.'

'Hi,' he said without interest. 'Francesca Heller?'

Jazz began to wonder if Francesca was being quite so unreasonable about Conrad Domitio after all.

'You mean my plain and prickly business partner?' she asked sweetly.

It seemed to Jazz that he suddenly saw her. Some of the fire in him abated.

'She told you that, did she?'

'She did.'

'Was she—I mean—she must have been upset.'

Jazz considered. 'Upset? We-ell. That's one way of putting it. I never heard her tell me to hold a man off with boat hooks before.'

Conrad took his time assimilating that. So it was unfortunate that Francesca came back from her trip to the coffee shop while he was still debating. She stopped dead in the doorway.

'What's he doing here?' She sent Jazz a burning look. 'I told you. I *told* you...'

And she marched straight out again.

Conrad looked after her blankly. 'What the hell...?'

'She won't be back until you've left,' Jazz told him kindly. 'She means it about the boat hooks.'

'Oh, this is ludicrous,' said Conrad. And strode out of the shop.

He caught up with her on the corner of the King's Road.

'OK. You want me to apologise? I apologise,' he said in a goaded voice.

Francesca was storming along, hardly noticing which way

she was going. Grovel, she thought. That's what he needed to do. Grovel at her feet. Apology did not begin to touch it.

'I don't want you to do one damned thing except leave me alone,' shouted Francesca.

'Don't be silly.'

'Don't patronise me,' she yelled.

'Then stop playing games.'

She was so full of rage she could hardly speak. 'I do— not—play—games.'

'No? Then why pretend we haven't met before? Was that for Daddy Heller's benefit or mine?'

'What?'

He was as angry as she was. But he was better at keeping it under control.

'Am I supposed to ignore the fact that the first time we met you denigrated my country, my family and my integrity? I don't hear you apologising for that.'

'The first…' Francesca broke off.

She stopped dead. Wood smoke. And pine. And the trembly, excited feeling of being on the edge of something momentous.

And his anger at his grandparents.

'Have we met before?'

'I don't know. You tell me. Have we?'

Of course she hadn't believed him. Of course, she hadn't. She had known in her bones, in her blood that he was the man from the balcony. Only she had managed to talk herself out of it, between her missing spectacles and her fear of behaving like a teenager.

She said in a voice like lead, 'You're the man from the balcony.'

'You took your time admitting that.'

'Why didn't you tell me?' Her voice didn't sound like her own. She was shaking inside.

'Why didn't you?' Conrad countered. His voice was perfectly normal. Furious but normal. He certainly wasn't shaking, inside or out.

She said, trying to convince herself, 'It was only a chat at a party. It wasn't *important*…'

He showed his teeth. 'You mean, not as important as the crown prince your daddy is going to buy you.'

She had been wrong to think he wasn't shaking, she saw. He was vibrating like a tuning fork. Only not with sexual awareness. None of her silly dreams for Crown Prince Conrad. He was quite simply a proud man who had been treated as if he was for sale. Francesca recognised that. At exactly the same time as she recognised that she had never seen anyone so angry in her whole life. An anger quite as great as his own leaped up to meet it.

'You—' He bit it off. *'Hell!'*

A red tide of rage crashed down over Francesca's head. If she had not had her hands full of paper cups of latte and espresso she would probably have regressed to childhood and hit out.

So she had no immediate means of defence when Conrad took her face between his gloved hands and kissed her hard.

For a moment—just a moment—it felt like heaven. It felt like coming home after a horrible journey.

It felt like love.

Then Francesca kicked him. And threw away the coffees. And ran.

It made a great photograph. Well, series of photographs really. The freelance, who had nearly given up on Crown Prince Conrad, in spite of the well-placed tip-off, thanked all the strange gods which paparazzi worship. And snapped away for the rest of the tumultuous two minutes. He even caught Francesca slamming the door to her bookshop so hard that a ten-book-high display stack in the window collapsed.

The tears glinting behind the glasses came out particularly well.

They were in two of the tabloid papers the next morning. In all the celebrity-watch magazines by the end of the week.

By the end of the month they were all over magazines in Europe and the States.

Francesca stopped answering her phone and never went out without a headscarf. It cost her a fortune in bottles of vodka, but the amused porters in her block barred entrance to the enterprising Press.

The Buzz got more customers in a week than it had had in the last three months.

Peter Heller gave a Press conference. He pledged a substantial sum to the presidential campaign fund of ex-King Felix and refused to be drawn on whether his daughter was dating the crown prince. The campaign promptly got into most of the Sunday newspapers in Europe. More funds flowed in.

And Conrad—well, Conrad was not talking. Not to anyone. Not the Press, or his family, or even the imperious Peter Heller. Conrad, he announced, was only willing to talk to one person.

Francesca.

CHAPTER FIVE

FRANCESCA refused to talk to him. 'I don't care what the papers say,' she said, untruthfully.

Her father said she owed it to herself. Ex-King Felix said she owed it to her country. The ex-queen—Francesca was coming to hate that woman—said she owed it to Conrad. Francesca resisted them all.

And then her mother took a hand.

'How clever of you, darling,' said Lady Anne, striding into the flat as if they had come face to face only yesterday, instead of Christmas, four months ago. 'I would never have thought you had it in you.'

She looked as if she had just come off the moor in her Barbour and headscarf. Or she would have done if it weren't for the priceless pearls and Peter Heller's knock-your-eyes-out diamond ring.

'Had what in me?' asked Francesca warily.

'Keeping a prince on a string. Especially Conrad Domitio. He used to be *so* glamorous. All the girls were after him. When he was young, of course. Before he became a dreary scientist. Now you've managed to make him look sexy again. Clever you.'

'Sexy!' Francesca was outraged.

Her mother bit back a smile. 'Of course. Everyone is saying you're breaking your heart for him. Nothing makes a man look so sexy as a heartbroken groupie.'

'*Groupie!*' Francesca nearly screamed.

'Isn't that what you call it when you've never actually been out with them?' asked Lady Anne innocently. 'But you know every last detail about them.'

'I do not...'

But, of course, she had let herself be trapped into snapping unwisely at one of the photographers. BEST-SELLING PRINCE ISN'T ACCESSIBLE ENOUGH, SAYS SAD FRAN had made her grind her teeth. What made it worse was that she knew it was all her own fault.

'Yes,' mused her mother. 'Sounded as if you had been hopelessly in love with him for years. You seemed to know so *much*.'

'Publishers' handout and paternal briefing,' said Francesca coldly. 'I'm in a unique position.'

'Yes. That's what the Press is saying,' agreed her mother, helping herself to coffee. 'Do you know, someone rang and asked me if you had his photo on your wall as a child?'

Francesca clutched her head. 'Do they think I'm a complete fool?'

Her mother sat down at the kitchen table and cupped her hands round the mug. 'They think you're a rich girl who can't get a man,' she said frankly. 'No point in dressing it up. And you helped them think it.'

Francesca was speechless.

Her mother swirled her coffee. 'I wonder if that Barry person will talk to them.'

Francesca's sense of humour reasserted itself. 'And tell them he did an audit of my stock holdings before he proposed? I don't think so.'

Her mother shook her head at her unworldly daughter. 'He doesn't have to tell them the truth,' she explained kindly. 'All he has to do is point out that you and he were seeing each other and are no longer an item. A hack who put his mind to it could do a lot with that. Make you look really desperate.' She savoured her coffee. 'Still, what do you care? You're a career woman with a successful business to run.'

Francesca found that she did not find that much of a consolation.

'It's all such a pack of lies,' she muttered.

'The camera cannot lie.'

'Huh!'

'Did Conrad make you cry or did he not?'

Francesca had looked at that hateful photograph so many times she could have drawn it from memory. But she could not claim that it had been doctored.

'With temper,' she said excusingly.

'Just like any rejected groupie.'

There was a long, fraught silence. Then Francesca stood up.

'I don't care whether people think I can't get a man. But I'm not having all my friends and relations thinking I'm an overheated stalker,' she said firmly. 'I'll talk to Conrad.'

Lady Anne pursed her lips. 'All the tabloid attention must be getting in the way of his work. Perhaps he just wants it all to go away. It could well be hopeless.'

Francesca's chin lifted.

Her mother bit back a smile. That was her Francesca: never accept that anything was hopeless.

'He'll talk to me,' said Francesca with resolution.

She still had a shopping list of requirements, after all. And to start it off Conrad had to grovel.

Conrad had given up hope of her returning his calls. He sat looking at the computer screen and trying not to think about her.

He was supposed to be reviewing a paper on the movement of tectonics sent to him by a colleague in Japan. He had read the same paragraph at least five times and he still couldn't remember what it said by the time he got to the end.

What was happening to him? Even when he and Silvia had been breaking up, he had never been unable to concentrate like this. Hell, he had *buried* himself in work while Silvia went off skiing and sunbathing and, eventually, marrying her handsome tennis coach. He had never picked over their conversations, word by word. He had never known what to do.

What had Francesca Heller done to him?

She haunted his dreams. Those toffee-brown eyes! That belligerent chin! But most of all, the thing he could not get out of his head, was the way she had trembled when he touched her on that sodden balcony. And again, when he kissed her.

She had kicked him. She had looked as if she was going to explode. She had damn nearly brought the bookshop down with her violent door-slamming. But she had trembled first. And her voice changed when he touched her.

His body clenched hard at the memory. He could have groaned aloud.

She would not admit it, of course. Hell, she might not even have realised it. But Conrad had lashings of experience, and he knew that little catch in the voice for what it was.

Damn her father for interfering! Damn Felix and all monarchists! Damn the book trade and her ambitious partner! Damn all the things that were getting in the way.

What he wanted to do was gather her up and take her off into the hills with him. No money, no monarchists, just themselves and the elements. He would make her stand up and fight for her own man, not get her daddy to buy her one.

And then he would take care of her. Oh, he would. He would make those soft brown eyes glow as they had glowed that first night when neither of them knew who they were talking to. When they just knew what they wanted...

His body was responding unmistakeably. Conrad gave a breathless laugh. He had to stop this. If just the memory of Francesca Heller could do this, he was in a lot deeper than he had been for a long time. He clenched his jaw.

'Not yet,' he said aloud. 'She's got to talk to me first.'

Of course she wouldn't talk to him. More than half of that was his own fault too, no matter how much he cursed Felix and Peter Heller. He should never have said she was plain and prickly. He could not think why he had done it—except that he was shaken by finding her at his grandfather's and apparently in the market for a husband with a title. It had thrown him into a worse temper than he could ever remember. Even so, that piece of schoolboy nastiness was not like him.

Cool, calm Prince Conrad! In control of everything! So sure of his ability to make everyone dance to his tune, he thought savagely. Not in control of his own tongue, though. Nor, by the drift of his present thoughts, wholly in control of his body either.

He punched his keyboard so hard that the computer beeped. 'You have performed an illegal operation,' the screen told him blandly.

Conrad bared his teeth at the message. 'I wish.'

Experience had taught him there was nothing to do but wait for the computer to shut down and then reboot. He tapped his fingers impatiently on the mouse mat.

'Life lesson,' he muttered. 'Sometimes there's nothing to do but wait.'

Especially as he did not have one single idea what to do next. He tried to comfort himself that sometimes situations just had to be left to brew. A solution would come to him. Conrad was a great believer in not forcing the pace.

The trouble was, his body did not agree with him, he thought wryly. But his body was just going to have to be patient. He had always been good at patience. Up to now, anyway.

He straightened his shoulders and applied himself to the Japanese professor's careful exposition of temperature changes at assorted boreholes.

So when she rang he was not prepared.

'This is Francesca Heller.' She sounded brisk.

His mouth dried. He could not think of anything to say.

'Hello? Hello?' Rather less brisk now. 'Is that Conrad Domitio's office?'

'Yes,' he said in a strangled voice.

'Can I talk to him, please?' Under the briskness, there was a little tremor of nervousness. He had heard it before.

His body recognised it before his brain did. He drew an eloquent breath. What was she doing to him?

He swallowed hard. 'Conrad Domitio speaking.'

'Oh!' He heard the catch in her voice. He could almost see the way those revealing eyes must be widening. She had had her speech prepared and now she could not remember a word of it. Conrad was certain of it.

How well I know her, he thought, startled. Better than I knew Silvia after three years of marriage.

Marriage!

And quite suddenly it was there, in his head, the whole picture. Forget fury, forget pride. He and Francesca Heller were made for each other.

There was only one possible solution. It would take time to convince her of it, of course. But he could do it. He *could* do it. He knew her; he knew himself; and he was patient and determined.

It would take time and she would fight him every step of the way. But in the end she would marry him. No other outcome was possible.

'Hello?' she said, even more uncertain.

He swallowed. This is where it starts. Operation Marrying Francesca.

He said carefully, gently, 'You took me by surprise. I wasn't expecting to hear from you.'

'Then it isn't true that you told my father you wouldn't talk to anyone but me? About this stuff in the papers, I mean.'

'Yes, it's true. I just didn't think you were—' he picked his words with care 'ready to talk.'

'Well, I am,' she said gruffly.

His heart leaped. For a moment he felt almost suffocated. 'Why?'

But it was not because of that overwhelming attraction. Of course it wasn't. She hadn't noticed that yet. It was going to be his extreme pleasure to awaken her to it. But not yet.

'Because they're saying I'm your groupie,' she was saying hardly. 'I don't want my friends to think I'm the next best thing to a stalker.'

'Ah.' Well, of course it had to be something like that. He was still shocked by the depth of his disappointment.

'Haven't you *seen* the Press?' She sounded impatient.

'No. I don't usually read the celebrity columns.'

'But when you're in them—'

'It's not the first time,' said Conrad drily 'It won't be the last. I don't need to be told what I'm doing and feeling. If it's true it's redundant. If it's lies it just gets me into a temper.'

There was a little silence. He could hear her assimilating that.

'You think temper's a bad thing?' she asked at last, wistfully.

'Waste of energy,' said Conrad, thinking how much better he could direct his energies if she were here.

'How calm you are.' It didn't sound as if she liked that. 'Doesn't it worry you the least little bit?'

'The only thing that has worried me is the thought that you might be having a hard time,' he said truthfully. 'Now, when and where do we meet?'

At once she tried to back off. He would have put money on her going into retreat as soon as he named a time and place, he thought affectionately. But in the end he gentled her into agreeing, almost without her realising. He even left her laughing when she cut the call.

Conrad put the phone down. He sat and stared at the thing for a full five minutes as if it had suddenly turned into a pumpkin. And then he spun and spun his chair round, punching the air.

'Yes!'

Quite suddenly the temperatures of pre-earth-tremor incidents were riveting. He flung himself back into work as if he had never even heard the words 'failure to concentrate'.

Francesca would not let him pick her up from the bookshop. She said it was in case one of the paparazzi picked them off. But that was not the real reason. She did not want Jazz to see them together.

She was not really sure why. Except that she knew that Jazz would say something worldly and sophisticated. Then she, Francesca, would have to laugh and say something worldly and sophisticated back. So when she went off with Conrad she

MILLS & BOON®

An Important Message from The Editors of Mills & Boon®

Dear Reader,

Because you've chosen to read one of our romance novels, we'd like to say "thank you"!

And, as a **special way** to thank you, we've selected <u>two more</u> of the <u>books</u> you love so much **and** a welcome gift to send you absolutely <u>FREE!</u>

Please enjoy them with our compliments...

Tessa Shapcott

Editor, Mills & Boon

P.S. And because we value our customers we've attached something extra inside...

EDITOR'S "THANK YOU" SEAL

PEEL OFF AND PLACE INSIDE

How to validate your Editor's Free Gift "Thank You'

1. **Peel off the Free Gift Seal** from the front cover. Place it in the space provided to the right. This automatically entitles you to receive two free books and a beautiful gold-plated Austrian crystal necklace.

2. **Complete your details** on the card, detach along the dotted line, and post it back to us. No stamp needed. We'll then send you two free novels from the Tender Romance™ series. These books have a retail value of £2.55, but are yours to keep absolutely free.

3. **Enjoy the read.** We hope that after receiving your free books you'll want to remain a subscriber. But the choice is yours - to continue or cancel, any time at all! So why not accept our no risk invitation? You'll be glad you did.

Your satisfaction is guaranteed

You're under no obligation to buy anything. We charge you nothing for your introductory parcel. And you don't have to make any minimum number of purchases – not even one! Thousands of readers have already discovered that the Reader Service™ is the most convenient way of enjoying the latest new romance novels before they are available in the shops. Of course, postage and packing to your home is completely FREE.

Tessa Shapcott
Editor, Mills & Boon

would already have got into a way of behaving which might not be—well—wise. Not in the circumstances. Possibly even downright dangerous. In the worldly and sophisticated stakes, Francesca acknowledged, Prince Conrad Domitio had her beaten hollow.

So she met him in the front entrance of the National Gallery. Even in the late spring it was full of tourists. Among such a crowd, no one was going to notice a short dark girl with glasses, clutching a catalogue like a magic amulet for protection, Francesca reasoned.

She was even right. Only she had, of course, reckoned without Conrad. People had been noticing Conrad since he was seventeen. These days, they stared. Even Francesca, hot and embarrassed and trying to hang on to her thirst for vengeance, could see why.

He strolled through the tall vestibule as if he had just come off the range. He was tall and lean in his black jeans. And he moved like an athlete. It was devastating.

The party of schoolgirls knew it. Two keen-eyed matronly art lovers knew it. Even the weary front-desk attendant knew it. Francesca, riveted to unfathomable dark eyes and a mouth she knew the schoolgirls were sighing over, gave a shiver of pure animal awareness.

Maybe…maybe this wasn't such a good idea after all…maybe she should just turn and run *now*…

But it was too late. He had seen her. And he was smiling. Suddenly that dangerous mouth looked a lot less sensual. The eyes were clear as daylight. Even sunny. But… But…

Careful, she said to herself.

She went forward, the catalogue clenched at her breast.

He did not try to kiss her. Francesca did not know whether she was glad or sorry about that. And he could not shake hands without wrenching the catalogue away from her. So they both nodded; she in acute discomfort, he easily.

In fact, Conrad looked as if he hardly noticed whether they touched or not. He was all courtesy and consideration.

'I kept you waiting. I'm sorry.'

The apology flustered her. 'No, no. I was early. Nothing to be sorry about.'

'That's a matter of opinion.' His eyes glinted down at her as if he was inviting her to share the joke.

Francesca swallowed. Not a subject she wanted to go into just now.

'Well…' she said lamely. 'Do you want to look at any of the pictures? Or shall we just go somewhere and talk?'

'Might as well see one or two, now we're here.'

Typically, he had no doubts which picture he wanted to see. Typically also, he knew the gallery layout and went straight to his favourite. And then knew all about the painting.

'There,' he said with satisfaction. '*Portrait of a Man*. Titian. Just look at that.'

Francesca did. 'Very striking,' she said politely.

He looked down at her, amused. 'Don't you like it?'

She shook her head. 'I don't know anything about Renaissance painting.'

She struggled to find something complimentary to say. In truth she did not like the picture very much at all. It was a portrait of a man in three-quarter profile, shown only from the waist upwards. He was gypsy-dark, with an aggressive tilt to his head and a look of physical toughness under the marvellously painted brocade and velvet. *I wouldn't like to cross him,* she thought. And remembered that she had once thought that of Conrad.

She swallowed and firmly turned her thoughts to brushwork and pigment.

'The sleeves are nice,' she offered.

Conrad flung back his head and roared with laughter.

'Does he unsettle you?' The dark, secretive face was alive with wicked mischief. Not unlike the cool thug in court dress on the wall. 'Now, why?'

Francesca measured the portrait. 'He doesn't look very kind.'

Conrad blinked. 'Kind? No, probably not. But so alive.' He strode backwards and forwards in front of the picture, restless and animated. 'Look at him. In theory he's leaning on that table or window sill or whatever it is. But actually he's ready to jump up and mix in at the first sign of trouble. You can see it.'

Was that like Conrad too? thought Francesca. How little she knew about him. And what about the fierce sexuality of the man in the picture? Yes, they shared that all right.

Under Conrad's lazily down-dropped lids, behind the easy stroll, there was masculinity as powerful as a forest fire. She did not quite know how she knew it was there. She had never really felt the force of it. But she knew she *could*. If one day Conrad decided that he wanted to stop playing games with her, no amount of civilised behaviour or paternal contacts were going to get her off the hook.

She looked at the portrait again and made a discovery. 'It's a challenge. The way he's looking at us. He's daring us to take him on.'

Conrad's eyebrows flew up. 'I've always thought that too,' he said slowly. 'But women don't usually see it, in my experience.'

Francesca was dry. 'Challenge is about the only body language I recognise, according to my mother.'

'Ah,' said Conrad, storing the information away for future use. And trying not to dwell too much on the implications just at the moment. Somewhat distractedly, he went on, 'Of course, it's not the viewers that he wants to take on. It's the painter.'

'But why sit for him if he didn't like him?'

He breathed gratefully. Nothing like a bit of art appreciation for curbing the libido, he thought with quick self-mockery.

'Liking's got nothing to do with it. It's chemistry, pure and simple.'

Francesca looked again. It did not help.

'Sorry, you've lost me.'

'Look at it this way. The guy is good at what he does. Successful. Young. It's a sexy package. And then he meets the painter. And the painter can *do something he can't*. He can paint. And when people come around they aren't going to say, Aren't you handsome? Aren't you rich?' He laughed softly 'What great sleeves! They're going to say, Titian is brilliant.'

'He's jealous?' Francesca said gropingly.

'No. No, of course not. He wants Titian to be brilliant. They're two of a kind. But by golly Titian had better *be* the best. They both have to be the best they can. So he pushes Titian all the time. Needles him. That's the challenge you say you see.'

Francesca said slowly, 'You've thought about this a lot, haven't you?'

'I like that picture. I always have.'

'No, not the picture. This challenge thing.'

'Ah. That.'

'Well?'

He stopped pacing and nodded slowly. 'I suppose I have.'

'You challenge people, don't you?'

His eyelids drooped suddenly. It was deceptively lazy but Francesca was sure, she did not know how, that his every sense was alert.

He took a long time answering. 'Sometimes.' It was a drawl.

'So was that what it was with me? At that horrible lunch party with all the lectures on your family tree? A challenge? Just a game after all?' She felt oddly bereft.

His eyes glinted down at her. How could she have thought they were dark? Now she was so close she could see that they were a strange greeny hazel.

Conrad said softly, 'I don't play games. My challenges are deadly serious.'

Francesca jumped as if she had touched a live wire.

She said uncertainly, 'So it wasn't a challenge? When you were so—'

'Nasty,' he supplied.

She gave a startled little laugh. 'Yes, that about covers it.'

He took her arm and led her away from the painting. 'That reminds me about the first thing I wanted to do.'

'Which was?'

'Grovel,' said Conrad with complete sang-froid.

Francesca jumped about a foot in the air. Could he read her mind?

'I was out of line. You weren't meant to hear what I said but even so. I'd never have said that you were prickly if I hadn't already been in a furious temper.'

'*Plain* and prickly,' Francesca reminded him darkly.

He was unrepentant. The charm enveloped her, like sun on one of the Renaissance Italian hillsides on the walls in front of them.

'Well, there you are. That goes to prove it was just the stupidity of the moment.'

She walked behind him in silence for a moment. Her thoughts were in turmoil. Grovelling was only a start, she reminded herself. Besides, she did not trust charm. She never had. Barry, she remembered with a little shock, had been very charming. Everyone said so.

She said, 'I wish I wasn't so bad at reading people.'

Conrad stopped dead and stared at her. Under the heavy lids his eyes were bright with interest.

'Bad at reading people?' he echoed.

Francesca gave a wry smile. 'All my life. I'm hopeless. My mother says it's because I'm too like my father.'

'And are you?'

'In some things.'

A straggle of tourists came towards them. They all held plastic stalks to their ears, clearly listening to a translation of the gallery tour. Between that and their jockeying position to get close to their guide, they blocked Francesca's way.

Conrad put an arm round her and drew her against his side as if he had been doing it all his life. She dropped her catalogue.

This time the electrical awareness was like a lightning streak. How could he not feel it? thought Francesca. She was actually having trouble breathing.

This was crazy. She was not some regency miss to faint every time a man laid a finger on her. Even when he let her go to pick up her catalogue, she could still feel his touch, like a brand, right through her.

But somehow Conrad made her feel as if she had a layer of skin missing. Or no, as if he could find his way under several layers of skin, which no one else knew how to do and he could traverse without even trying.

Oh, boy, am I out of my depth, thought Francesca, accepting her catalogue distractedly. Barry had never made her sizzle just by putting an arm round her waist. And this was a clothed arm round her trousered and jacketed waist. Yet she felt as if he had put a hand on her naked skin.

Or, look at it another way, as feverish as a pre-teen when her pop-star idol blew her a kiss. That is ludicrous, she told herself, trying to be brisk.

Get a grip, Francesca. You're too old for this sort of nonsense.

He said, 'It's getting full, isn't it? Want to go somewhere with less traffic?'

She swallowed. 'Yes, please.'

He walked her through Trafalgar Square. He didn't touch her again.

He took her into a small, bright café and bought her coffee. The place was full of tourists, chattering in at least five languages, scanning maps, writing postcards. All oblivious of the couple in the corner.

And that's what we feel like. A couple.

The thought came out of nowhere. Francesca flinched. Only three weeks ago you thought you and Barry were a couple, she reminded herself. Just how fickle was she?

He pushed aside a newspaper that someone had left on the table, and pushed the sugar towards her. All of a sudden he looked very serious.

'Look—do you think we could start again?'

Francesca did not know what to say. So she said nothing.

'I know it's a lot to ask.' A smile flickered. 'I'd turn me down in your place. But—this is not just about me.'

Of course, thought Francesca, struck to the heart. He would

not have wanted to see her again because he wanted to see her again. Not a world-class lust object like Prince Conrad Domitio.

Oddly, it was almost a relief. She stopped being tongue-tied.

'I think you'd better explain.' Oh, she sounded so cool, so composed. Francesca was proud of herself.

He hesitated. 'I promised my grandfather...' he said, almost to himself. 'You see, Felix is very committed to Montassurro. I don't know if you can understand that. He feels guilty about fleeing. Though he was only seventeen and would have been shot if he'd stayed. Everyone wanted him to go. He was supposed to be the figurehead of the opposition in exile. Just nobody expected that it would take damn nearly fifty years for the communist regime to fall. In the meantime, life was bad in Montassurro for most people. Felix did what he could— sent aid, helped refugees—but basically he thinks he should have been there to share the hardships.'

Francesca frowned. 'So?'

'Well, now he figures that he has a chance to make up for that.'

'You mean he wants to salvage his conscience by showering them with gifts. And wants my father to pay for it,' she interpreted.

He frowned. 'You're right, you *are* like your father. That's exactly the sort of thing Heller would say.'

She lifted her chin. 'I'm not ashamed of it.'

Their eyes clashed.

She said, 'Anyway, it's true. He's buying you a travelling hospital truck, isn't he?'

He looked at her for a long, steady moment. Then he said gently, 'He's buying Montassurro a hospital truck.'

She shrugged. 'Same difference.'

'You are so wrong.' It was so soft, it was almost menacing. But Francesca had the oddest feeling that he was angrier with himself than he was with her. Or even with her father.

He straightened his shoulders and said curtly, 'Montassurro

has been run by a bunch of gunrunners and profiteers ever since the communists fell. No doubt your father can tell you all about that. Now there are going to be elections. Felix is running for president. He wants —'

'Campaign funds. I know. My father's already made a public donation.'

He gave an exasperated sigh. 'Do you never think about anything but money? He wants your father's support.'

Francesca did not say anything. But she managed to look sufficiently sceptical to make his brows twitch together in a frown.

'Your father was a refugee,' he said curtly. 'So was Felix, once. Now they think they can do something to help. Is that so impossible to believe?'

There was no answer to that.

Well, there was, thought Francesca mutinously. But she wasn't going to say to him, My father wants to buy me a classy husband. And he thinks a Montassurran hospital truck is the price. Was she?

So she muttered, 'I suppose not,' and concentrated on stirring coffee that didn't need it.

He said more gently, 'I know we started off on the wrong foot.'

She looked up at that. 'We?'

He flung up his hands in a gesture of surrender. 'OK. I did. I didn't like what I knew of your father's business dealings, I admit it. I didn't like Felix trying to force my hand, either. At that lunch party I meant to be nasty. And I was. But I never meant to hurt your feelings like that.'

Francesca flinched inwardly. But she said with spirit, 'You didn't. And I didn't like having my hand forced either.'

'No. I can see that now.' He did not sound happy about it.

'So now you've apologised, that's all right, then. I forgive you. You forgive me. We don't have to see each other again.' Why did that feel like the end of the world? She said hardly, 'We can tell the elderlies to forget all about their stupid matchmaking. And tell the Press it's off.'

He hesitated.

Francesca's head reared up like a horse scenting battle. 'Can't we? Isn't that what this meeting's about?'

He gave that slow smile that, if she let it, turned her bones to water. 'Not exactly.'

She sat very still.

'I want you,' he said carefully, 'to say you'll marry me.'

You would have thought he'd shot her, Conrad thought, rather put out. His clever strategy was not supposed to get a reaction like this.

He had thought he was prepared for anything. She might storm off, furious. She might laugh him out of court. She might even, though something in his bones told him she would fight against it, find the idea exciting.

It had never occurred to him that she would sit and stare at him like a frozen computer screen. She did not blink for a full minute.

And then she said, 'Are you out of your mind?'

Well, at least that was closer to one of the reactions he had prepared for.

'No. Just being practical.'

'Practical!'

He said rapidly, 'Two main reasons. One: it gets Felix the feel-good spin that his campaign needs. And two: it gets you and me out of the clutches of the paparazzi.'

Her face had gone thin and hostile. 'What feel-good spin?'

'Everybody loves a lover. If one of the lovers is royal and the other is heiress to the richest man in the world, we have a fairy tale,' he said fluently.

'My father's not the richest man in the world,' she objected.

Conrad grinned. 'He will be by the time the staff writers have finished with the story.'

She did not think it was funny. 'Even so, what does that have to do with—' she boggled over what to call Felix. Conrad watched in deep appreciation as she settled on '—your grand-father?'

He shrugged. 'Search me, but it does. Ever since you and

I have been starring in the celebrity mags, his campaign is getting real coverage. People seem to be taking his manifesto seriously at last. Crazy!'

Her hostility diminished visibly. Out of academic interest, it seemed. 'It's called brand recognition.'

He blinked. 'What?'

She laughed, all hostility vanishing. Her eyes lit to gold when she laughed, Conrad saw. He watched, fascinated.

'I did ten weeks in an advertising agency once. Longest job I ever had until the bookshop. Half the secret of selling things to people is to give them the idea they've known the product for years. That's brand recognition. Oh, and then you have to make it seem all warm and fuzzy, of course.'

Conrad resisted the temptation to shudder by a supreme exercise of self-control. Nobody had ever—even by implication—called him warm and fuzzy before.

She made a decision. 'All right. I'll buy the spin argument. So why would getting engaged to you help me get away from a lot of stupid gossip columnists?'

Conrad took his time about answering. This was the big one.

'Have you ever had the paparazzi after you before?' he said at last.

Francesca bit her lip. 'Yes,' she admitted. 'Hence the fractured employment record. But it's never been like this.'

Conrad nodded. 'I know. Believe me, telling them there is no story is not an option. It will only make them keener.'

He watched her from under down-dropped lids. As she struggled to get her head round this unwelcome information she worried away at her bottom lip. He wanted to lean forward and stop her. He wanted to put a finger on her rosy mouth and say, 'Don't do that. You're hurting yourself.' He wanted—

Be honest Conrad, he told himself ironically. This is not altruism. You want to be kissing that luscious mouth.

Her eyes went dark as molasses when she concentrated.

Would they change yet again if he leaned forward and kissed her? And would she keep her eyes open or—?

Stop it! he told himself firmly. This is not part of the strategy. You'll find out what she does when she kisses you all in good time. First things first. You still have to convince her.

He said in his most casual tone, 'Look at it this way. As long as we deny it, they've got a story. We put our hands up to it and pfft! We're just one more boring engaged couple.'

Her teeth jabbed down involuntarily on her lower lip.

Ouch! he thought. But encouraging.

Well, maybe. It would be encouraging in other women. But Francesca Heller was not like other women.

'What I suggest is, we say, OK, you got us. Announce the engagement at the hospital ball. Let them take all the photographs they want. Then let all the fuss die down.'

She was frowning hard. 'Do you really think they'll leave us alone after that?'

He was not very honest but he was too honest for that.

'Not at first, no. But eventually, yeah, sure. Another story will come along. In the meantime, they'll have got lots of pretty pictures of you and me and your engagement ring.'

She jumped. Startled eyes flew to his.

Careful, Conrad. Getting too close! Back off fast.

'Don't worry. You can give it back afterwards if it makes you feel uncomfortable.'

She shook her head. 'It's not that.'

'What, then?'

A faint colour rose in her cheeks. 'I've never been engaged. It seems like bad luck to do it for the first time as a trick.'

He was utterly taken aback. For a moment he could not think of anything to say.

She did not seem to notice. She said with difficulty, 'You see, it was only a few weeks ago that I thought I was— Well, that doesn't matter.'

Yes, it does, he thought. He watched the way her fingers twisted and twisted the plastic spoon. It matters a lot. For the first time it occurred to him to wonder about previous men in her life. He didn't like it.

She seemed to notice the spoon suddenly—and how it was giving her away. She flung it down as if it had burned her. She stuck her chin in the air.

'I'm not good at relationships,' she announced belligerently.

For the second time in their conversation Conrad could not think of anything to say.

'I tend to say what I mean,' she went on, after a moment. 'I don't read body language. And I have absolutely no tact.'

A smile dawned. 'Sounds like the perfect woman.'

She sent him a look of dislike. 'You're missing the point. It makes me a terrible liar. I'm not going to be any good as a pretend fiancée. I'll keep forgetting.'

'Ah.'

'And the moment anyone asks me something concrete, like if we've set a date for the wedding or where we're going to live, I'll just fall apart.'

Conrad looked at her. She was seriously upset, he saw. The hot-toffee eyes were suspiciously misty, even behind the glasses. He had seen that misty-eyed look before, but last time, he'd now realised, it was because she couldn't see properly. Now he thought there was another reason for it.

To his own astonishment, he put out a hand and covered hers.

'Hey, don't look like that. No one's going to try and talk you into doing anything you don't want to.'

Now, why did he say that? That was exactly what he was supposed to be doing.

She swallowed. 'I'm sorry.'

'Don't be. You're entitled to tell the truth if you want to.'

Francesca gave a watery chuckle. 'That's big of you.'

'You have no idea how big,' he said involuntarily.

It disconcerted her. Her eyes flared warily. 'What?'

'Nothing. Tell me instead about the man you *want* to get engaged to.' Now, why had he said that? It was the last thing he wanted to hear about.

And he was crazily relieved when she shook her head and said, 'Wanted. Barry is strictly past tense. Another one of my thumping mistakes.'

She was trying to make a joke out of it but Conrad saw there was more to it than that. He resisted the urge to cup her face comfortingly. Just.

'Want to talk about it?'

She shook her head again. Violently this time. 'Nope. Learned my lesson. Drawn a line under it. Move on. That's my philosophy.'

But her brave words were at odds with those wounded eyes.

He said slowly, 'So he's definitely history and you're ready to move on.'

She swallowed again. 'Yes,' she said. She sounded as if she was volunteering to go into battle.

'If you're sure…'

'I am. Definitely. Barry de la Touche is off my Christmas-card list permanently.'

He noted the name but now was not the time to talk about anyone else. Instead he gave her the long, slow smile that invited her to join him in mischief.

'Then I think I may have a solution.'

That startled her. 'What?'

'Forget all this nonsense about pretend engagements and stories for the Press. We're both adults. We're both single. We have no commitments. Let's do it for real.'

CHAPTER SIX

'YOU'RE crazy,' said Francesca.

She went on saying it. Right up until he left to give a lecture at the Earth Sciences Museum. And then later when he called. And the next day. And the next.

'Don't you ever give up?' she said, exasperated, after a week of evening phone calls.

'Do you?'

'Not often,' she had to admit.

'Something else we have in common, then.' He sounded smug.

'What was the first thing?' she said coldly. 'I seem to have missed that.'

He chuckled. 'The ability to recognise a challenge.'

She didn't trust him an inch. So tall, so charming. So confident of his charm.

It worked too, dammit. He got her to laugh every time. She could hear him smiling down the phone when she finally succumbed to giggles.

Francesca strove hard to remember that she wanted to wipe that superior smile off his face. Crown Prince Conrad was an arrogant snob, she told herself. A time-server, too.

He thought she was plain and prickly until it suited him to fancy marrying her. And he had castigated her father as a crook. She had been right when she wanted his total public defeat. The only problem was that she had about as much likelihood of bringing it about as she had of reaching the moon.

'Oh, I recognise a challenge all right,' she said with grim private humour.

Conrad was as quick as a cat, even at the other end of a

telephone. 'Sounds intriguing,' he said. 'Something I can help with?'

She gave a snort of laughter, quickly suppressed.

'Ah. My head on a charger,' he said, interpreting easily. 'I've commented on this unforgiving tendency in you before.'

She took the battle into his court. 'Do you blame me? You were vile all through that horrible lunch party.'

'You were pretty sharp, yourself. And at least I apologised.'

'Words are cheap,' she said darkly.

'Oh, you want deeds, do you?' He sounded amused. 'All right. Set me a task. If I complete it, you marry me. Deal?'

'Oh, grow up,' said Francesca, disconcerted at last. She banged the phone down.

But when he rang back the next night she was ready for him. She had even written out her shopping list.

'Right,' she said. 'First of all you've got to be nice to my father. I mean really nice. No looking down your nose and making cracks about his Ferraris.'

'You drive a hard bargain,' complained Conrad. 'I'll try. What else?'

She was biding her time on getting him to admit the deficiencies of his grandparents. But she could force him to tell the truth about dodgy royalty in general. She knew how, too.

'Admit to me that you traded on your title to get that damned book published.'

There was a blank pause.

'Excuse me?' said Conrad frostily.

'The volcano thing with the pictures.'

'I suggest you read it. Then ask me that again, if you dare.' And it was his turn to slam the phone down.

So Jazz found her surreptitiously sidling into the popular-science area next morning.

'If you're looking for Prince Charming's book, it's on order,' Jazz said helpfully. 'We've sold out.'

Francesca leaped guiltily. 'No, no. I was just interested in what was hot at the moment.' She grabbed several kilos of reading matter on the genome project and headed for the till.

'I just bet you are,' said Jazz with a grin. She relented. 'I'll lend you my copy if you promise to give it back without chocolatey fingerprints or tear stains. It may be a bit alarming if you actually know the guy.'

Francesca fulminated but she accepted the offer. Still, 'I'm not likely to weep over a book about seismology,' she said haughtily.

But she was wrong.

Conrad had largely transposed it from his expedition diary. He was an economical writer, especially when it came to his own exploits. The contrast between his matter-of-fact account and the terrifying photographs made Francesca's heart leap into her mouth.

When he called that night she said at once, 'I'm sorry. I should never have said that about the book. It's extraordinary.'

'Thank you.' He sounded genuinely pleased. 'Though I admit the publishers love my being a crown prince. It's just me that thinks it's irrelevant.'

Francesca had to accept that he meant that, at least.

'So now will you marry me?'

'No.'

He sighed. 'What else have I got to do?'

She grinned, unseen. He was going to have to recant on the plain and prickly assessment. But that would take time and considerable effort on her own part. In the meantime…

'You have to admit that Montassurran mead is filthy and no one in their right mind would drink it unless they had to,' she announced with pleasure.

'You're not serious.'

'Oh, but I am.'

'This is treason.'

'This is the taste buds fighting back,' she corrected.

His voice was wickedly teasing. 'It was my attar of roses you didn't like, wasn't it? What have you got against aphrodisiacs?'

Francesca choked and slammed the phone down.

The next day a parcel arrived at the shop, special delivery, for the personal attention of Ms Heller. It looked about the size of a book. She did not pay much attention to it. She did not even open it until mid-afternoon, when they had a quiet spell.

When she did she let out a muffled cry and dropped it.

Jazz strolled over. She looked at the contents of the parcel with mild surprise.

'Someone sending you a parcel bomb disguised as a night-time drink? What will these publicity people think of next? Which book is it advertising?'

'It's not from a publisher,' said Francesca, clutching the fat little jar to her breast. She was almost certain that her ears were pink.

'So who's sending you cocoa? Doesn't sound like your mum somehow. Now, if it were *my* mum— Ah, here's a card.' She broke off to read it. 'Blimey.'

She held out the card. Francesca snatched it.

' "Guaranteed aphrodisiac-free. Sweet dreams," ' she read. *'Oh!'*

'I'm not even going to ask,' said Jazz, grinning.

Francesca ground her teeth and pointedly returned Conrad's book to her.

'I suppose you thought that was very funny,' she said to Conrad when he called that night.

'Yup.'

'What would have happened if the Press had got hold of it? They keep popping up at the bookshop like a rash that won't go away.'

'We tell them to mind their own business.'

She was scornful. 'Much use that would have been if they'd seen your card. You do realise, that would have convinced them we were sleeping together?'

'Mmm. Let's do that for real too,' he said outrageously.

Francesca nearly dropped the phone, so unexpected, so sudden, so absolutely vivid was the image his words conjured up.

It made her feel like putty in his hands. Just like Barry, she thought, cringeing. What a fool they must think I am. All desire to laugh left her.

'Francesca? Are you there?'

She rallied. 'Yes, I'm here.'

His tone was concerned. 'What is it?'

'Nothing. I—just knocked a book off the table,' she said, fabricating wildly.

But she changed the subject fast. And went on doing so, from then on, every time he tried to take the conversation onto a more intimate plane. She told him about her numerous jobs, her volatile parents, the fun she was having at The Buzz. She did not tell him about Barry. But then, he never asked.

He told her about what it was like to be a seismologist. 'Most of the time you're locked to a computer. Just sometimes they let you out. Then you climb into dark holes and tap rocks. My father always said it was inevitable. It was the only job I was going to get where I was allowed to get dirty and dangerous and make a lot of noise at the same time.'

Bad as she was at reading people, she was still pretty sure that he had liked his father a lot. Both his parents had been drowned in a boating accident when Conrad was twenty. 'Bad scene,' he said briefly. He never reverted to the subject and Francesca was too self-conscious to ask. It clearly still hurt and she was, she thought, too clumsy with people's feelings to risk it. It was such an intimate thing to pursue.

And they were not intimate. Of course they were not. She was seeing to it.

But then Peter Heller rang and said that Conrad had asked him up to Cambridge and given him a very pleasant tour of the town, ending with dinner in one of the colleges as a guest of a friend of Conrad's.

'Interesting people. Very intelligent. They have asked me to go to a chess match with them,' said Peter with satisfaction. 'You are invited also. He told me to ask you particularly.'

So that part of her commission was fulfilled, thought Francesca. Her heart fluttered. Was it possible that one day Conrad might really turn up on the doorstep with all her tasks fulfilled, demanding that they get engaged? And for real?

He did not. But he did offer to do an author's reading evening at the bookshop and, when he turned up, made it plain that this was a personal favour to Francesca. It was the only reading he did to promote *Ash on the Wind*. And so he kept telling everyone.

The reading drew a huge crowd. Even Jazz raised her eyebrows at the length of the queue at the till after his talk. Several photographers got off some good shots of Conrad with his arm round Francesca. And there was a particularly telling one of him smiling at her over the heads of fans who wanted his signature on the book.

Francesca saw it with misgiving. What was the good of telling herself they weren't intimate, when there were photographs like that in every tabloid newspaper? Photographs that said the exact reverse!

And he sent her roses. A whole box full of them, to the shop the day after the author reading. The card read, 'Have some roses you don't have to drink. The rest we can talk about...'

'A silly joke,' she said repressively to a knowing look from Jazz.

But still she took the flowers home with her, walking along to her riverside apartment in the spring twilight, clutching them to her like a child's Christmas doll, and trying to curb a tendency to skip. She didn't want passers-by to think she was mad.

Yet even so, she was astonished when he turned up on her doorstep later that night.

Par for the course, she thought, berating herself. Any normal woman would have seen it coming, she supposed.

Francesca was so far from seeing it coming that she decided to turn out the spare room at last and unload all the detritus of the last year. It stopped her listening for the phone like a lovesick teenager. Or a groupie, as her mother had so unforgivably called her.

There was no warning from the porter's desk; no preliminary beep from the entry phone outside. Just a brisk press on the bell in the corridor.

Francesca opened the door of the flat, expecting it to be one of the maintenance staff. She was as scruffy as she could be, brown hair scragged up in a ragged pony-tail and her face flushed and dirty from house cleaning. She was barefoot too and clasping a broom. Her hands were encased in bright turquoise rubber gloves.

It was a long way from Paris fashion or even the neat business clothes in which he had seen her before. A long way, too, from what she had promised herself. One day he was going to look at her and find her beautiful. So beautiful it would blow him away. He would regret bitterly that he had ever called her plain. She had resolved it; she was just not quite sure how to bring it about. But, anyway, it was sure as hell not going to be tonight.

Conrad froze at the sight. His eyebrows flew up in comical astonishment.

'Oh, no,' wailed Francesca.

She tried to hide the broom, the rubber gloves and the bare feet in one mad contortionist's writhe. She failed.

He took the broom away from her helpfully.

'There goes my opening line,' he said with resignation.

She was so startled she stopped plucking helplessly at the rubber gloves. 'What?'

'I was going to say I hope this isn't an inconvenient time.'

'Oh.' She laughed, oddly relieved at the normality of it.

He was looking so gorgeous, she thought distractedly. All contained muscularity under the olive shirt and dark chinos. And his eyes were laughing. They were green, she discovered, sunny, luminous green; how could she ever have thought they were any sort of brown?

'Is this the spring cleaning I hear rumours of?'

'Er—no.' Actually she was getting rid of the last of the stuff that Barry had forgotten but she was not going to tell him that. 'Well, yes, I suppose. This week's featured non-fiction is about how to get rid of the clutter in your life.'

She was chattering. She knew she was chattering. But there was something about the intent look in those strange, amused eyes that rattled her badly.

'It said, start with the clutter in your home,' said Francesca with phoney brightness, still plucking ineffectually at her turquoise fingers. 'So I thought—why not? I— What are you doing?'

He had taken her wrist. At once her pulses went into flamenco rhythm. He smiled at her. Straight into her eyes. She was almost dizzy with what she saw there. Or was she mistaken again? As usual?

'Taking off your gloves,' he said blandly. 'Since they seem to be giving you trouble.'

Was it only her fevered imagination that detected a promise? A promise that the gloves were only the first of many things he would take off. She swallowed hard and hoped it wasn't audible. But she was almost certain it was.

He peeled the horrible things off efficiently. Much, much too slowly to keep her blood pressure stable, though. This was not *fair*.

She took her hands back.

'Thank you.'

Those unexpectedly green eyes gleamed. 'My pleasure.'

She believed him.

She thought: I am not sixteen. I am not a groupie. And I will *not* blush.

'Well, as you're here, you'd better come in,' she said ungraciously. She closed the door behind him. 'Can I give you a drink? Wine? Beer? No mead, on principle.'

He surprised her. 'That's a relief. I drink that stuff until my teeth curl when I'm with Felix. Don't need it anywhere else.'

Did that mean that the last of the tasks she had set him was completed? Francesca hovered between hope and panic. With a good dash of simple embarrassment.

But then he said in a matter-of-fact tone, 'Wine will be fine.'

So it was all in her fevered imagination, after all!

He followed her into the kitchen. Francesca made a great business of consulting her wine rack.

'Rioja? Chilean Cabernet Sauvignon? Or would you rather have white? There's Chablis. Australian Semillon? Sauvignon blanc?'

Conrad was patently uninterested. 'Whatever's open.'

Francesca straightened and looked him in the eye, through

severely smeared glasses. 'Nothing's open. I don't drink on my own.'

His eyebrows flew up. 'Oh, well, the Rioja, then.'

She extracted the bottle and began to scrabble at the foil over the cork. He gave her back the turquoise gloves and took the bottle away from her. He had the foil off in seconds and held his hand out for the corkscrew.

'I was hoping to persuade you to come out to dinner with me. Any chance?'

Of course there was no chance. Her hair was filthy, her fingernails were black and it would take her hours to get the accumulated dust and sticky residue of her cleaning activities off her skin.

She gave him the corkscrew and heard herself say, 'Thank you. That would be very nice.' And then, much too late, 'Why?'

Conrad removed the cork with the ease of long practice. He smelled it. 'That's OK. No rotten eggs. Glasses?'

Francesca hooked them out of the kitchen cupboard.

'Why?' she repeated on a rising note. Panic, suspicion, hope against hope—it was all there.

He poured wine into both glasses, put hers into her grubby paw and toasted her with his own.

'Because I want to have another shot at talking you into marrying me,' he said with complete sang-froid.

Francesca gasped. She was drinking Rioja at the time. An unpleasant few moments ensued.

Conrad thumped her on the back. When that failed he ran some water into a mug that she had left on the draining board and gave her that. His attempt at sympathy was undermined by the fact that he could not contain his laughter.

Francesca coughed until her eyes watered. She decided she hated him. She was certainly never, ever going to marry him.

'All right,' she said, when she could speak. 'Sell it to me.' Her glare dared him to do just that.

But it was the closest she came to saying no. To anything. She said yes to going out to a meal, though her stomach was much too knotted for food. She even took a quick shower, though what she really wanted was a long, hot bath. At least she would have done if she had not been so horribly conscious of him in the apartment beyond the bathroom door. She really didn't want to be naked any longer than was strictly necessary. And not because she thought he would break in on her either. It was entirely to do with the overheating of her own imagination.

'In fact, he's probably out there prowling through the book shelves, analysing your reading matter,' she told the flushed face in the bathroom mirror.

But when she emerged, hair still damp, it was not her taste in reading that he queried. He held up a man's tie. He was not smiling. And suddenly his eyes were hazel again.

'I thought you said he was in the past tense?'

Francesca snatched the tie. 'I never said I was a decent housekeeper, though. Where did you find it?'

'Down the back of a cushion on the sofa.'

'Oh.' She winced.

She remembered all too clearly now. It was the night Barry had asked her to marry him. They had ended up with their clothes half off, winding round each other while cushions fell and table lamps trembled. She had only just retained enough sanity to refuse to give him his answer straight away. And Barry had left.

She had thought it was because he was taking care of her. That, chivalrously, he would not use sex to pressure her into marriage. Chivalry! Huh! What an idiot she had been! What a trusting, naïve idiot!

She marched out into the kitchen and pushed the tie into the waste disposal with jerky movements. She switched it on and the thing nearly shook the sink to pieces, chewing up the last trace of Barry in the flat.

Then she swung round. Conrad was standing in the doorway, watching her gravely. She braced herself against the kitchen unit as if she was facing a firing squad.

'Well?' It was a challenge, chin raised.

'He hurt you.'

She shrugged. 'Not terminally.'

He took no notice of that. 'Are you still in love with him?' He sounded disturbed.

More disturbed than she would have expected.

'What does it matter to you?'

'Of course it matters. If you're still breaking your heart over Barry de la Touche it's going to cause complications to say the least.'

Complications? Was that all? Just as well she already knew the reasons behind that proposal of his, or she might be hurt all over again.

'I'm not,' she said curtly.

Conrad came into the kitchen and took her chin between his finger and thumb. He looked at her searchingly.

'Sure?'

'Of course I'm sure,' snapped Francesca. 'I'm no romantic heroine. My heart doesn't break. It's a bit bruised, that's all. But nothing like as bruised as my ego.'

He laughed at that. But she still caught him looking at her with concern as they left the apartment for dinner. And his eyes stayed hazel-dark for the rest of the evening.

Not that he was not a charming companion. He took her to an expensively quiet restaurant and lavished her with delicacies. He made her smile with his tales of his eccentric upbringing. And when he described his naughty Saturday-morning pupils he had her laughing aloud.

'Why on earth would one teach children that young about earthquakes?'

Conrad shook his head. 'Not earthquakes. The Montassurran language. Our cultural heritage.'

'Good heavens,' said Francesca blankly. 'I didn't know there was anywhere you could learn it. Except Montassurro, of course.'

'Well, for three hours on a Saturday morning St Catherine's Junior turns into an outpost of Montassurro.'

'Oh, great. Mead and brigandage! I wouldn't have thought there was a lot of call for either in the modern world. Why do people bother?'

There was a pause. Then he said quietly, 'Refugees salvage what they can.'

She felt rebuked. Her eyes fell. She felt she ought to apologise and did not know how. So she said nothing. And hated herself.

Conrad said in a level voice, 'You'll find most immigrant groups do it, one way or another. Some of them, like my grandfather, hope to go back one day. Others just want the children to be able to speak the same language as their grandparents.'

She struggled to find something neutral to say. 'Is that why you teach it?'

'I didn't get a vote. I inherited the obligation.'

She could not tell from his tone whether he accepted it gladly or resented it. An ordinarily sensitive woman would have been able to tell, she thought. But then, an ordinarily sensitive woman would have known that the language thing was important and not made a joke of it in the first place.

She could have kicked herself. Or cried. Or screamed.

Instead she did what she always did when faced with her own deficiencies. She changed the subject.

'Is it easy? As a language, I mean.'

He was surprised into laughing. 'Montassurran? Frankly, it's a bit of a dinosaur, since you ask. A bastard dinosaur. Fifty per cent Slav. Forty per cent Latin.'

'And the other ten per cent?' asked Francesca, the stickler for precision.

His mouth tilted wickedly. 'Pure caveman.'

Abruptly, she stopped hating herself. She looked at the glinting eyes and thought, *This man is seriously sexy. I could fall for him in a big way.*

And then, *Heck, I am already falling for him. Mayday! Mayday!*

Aloud she said, 'Caveman?'

His laughter bubbled over. 'Yes, that's right. Quite literally, apparently. Linguists get really excited about it.'

'But—*caveman?*'

'That may be a bit of an exaggeration. But the mountains

have been continuously inhabited for a very long time. It was even said that there were cave paintings, but they're lost now.'

'How can you lose a cave painting?' said Francesca scornfully. 'It's not as if someone's going to walk away with a rock wall.'

'No, but you can shut off the caves and make them a military training ground,' he said, his laughter dimming. 'Then you either blow them up on military exercises. Or you just forget where they were.'

'Oh.'

'You have no idea how much tradition the communist government wiped out, especially in the early years. They wanted to modernise at all costs. Felix says it cost them the soul of the mountains.'

Francesca recoiled from the over-dramatic phrase. 'Soul of the mountains? Oh, please.'

Conrad sighed. 'I know. I can't get my head round it either. But he really believes it. And so do the people who want him back. Of course, they also want his business expertise and his international contacts. And Felix feels it's a debt he's owed for a long time.' He stopped speaking. But he might just as well have carried on. The unspoken question hung in the air.

It was left to her to voice it.

'And you think I ought to pile in and help,' said Francesca, mock-resigned.

He leaned forward, suddenly eager.

'Here's the deal. We get engaged. For real, like you said. No pretence, open mind, we take it as it comes.'

Involuntarily she thought, *If only...* And shocked herself with the fierceness of it.

Conrad did not notice. 'We go to the hospital ball. Make the announcement. Get on with our lives. You have a job. I have a job. I travel a lot and I'll be in Montassurro for a month this summer, taking the first mobile-hospital unit into the mountains. We don't change any of that. But when I'm in England and you're not stocktaking at the shop we'll just date like an ordinary couple.'

Francesca stared at him incredulously. 'Ordinary couple?

Who are you kidding? We aren't ordinary. And we aren't a couple.'

It did not phase him one bit. 'We could be. And nobody's ordinary, if you think about it.'

'Neat,' she said ironically.

He acknowledged that as if she had meant it as a compliment.

'All you would have to do is come with me to the official functions. There are about three in the rest of the year. I'll let you have the dates and some notes nearer the time.'

'Great. Parties with briefing notes,' muttered Francesca. 'You're sure that's all I'd have to do?'

'Anything else is entirely up to you and me. Whatever you usually do on dates.'

She was not rising to that one. She stuck her chin in the air and dared him to bring up cocoa or roses. 'Such as?'

He hesitated. Then an odd smile flickered.

'Well, let me woo you, of course.'

She nearly bounced out of her chair. *What?*

The smile disappeared. Steep lids dropped. When the brilliant eyes were unveiled he looked almost bored.

'You were the one who said you didn't want a pretend engagement.'

'I didn't mean I wanted you to... I mean, you don't have to...' She was floundering. She pulled herself together. 'The whole idea is preposterous.'

'No, it isn't. We can have a pretend engagement. Or I woo you. There's no halfway house.'

'I could forget the whole thing and go home now,' flashed Francesca. She was horribly upset and she did not know why.

His eyes lifted. 'Could you?'

She thought of the Saturday-morning language classes. Of Felix struggling to compensate for escaping from his homeland sixty years ago. Of lost cave paintings. Above all, of mountain villages with no medical care and a man who was going to take time out to take them a mobile hospital.

'No,' she said on a little puff of anger and frustration. 'No,

I can't. I suppose I'll have to do my bit. I'm half-Montassurran, after all.'

There was a small silence. She had the odd feeling that he was disappointed somehow.

But then he said smoothly, 'So we're agreed, then.'

And she realised she must have been mistaken. Again!

He walked her back to her apartment. It was a clear night but cool and the streets were almost empty. He took her hand.

Francesca jumped, swallowed, curbed her instinct to wrench it away—and felt like a fool. Her hand felt the size of a baseball mitt. She felt as if she was one burning blush all the way from her hairline to her toes.

Get a grip, she told herself feverishly.

And thanked God that the sodium glare of the street lighting leached all colour out of both of them. So at least he wouldn't see that she was scarlet with embarrassment.

He could feel how uptight she was, though. There was no disguising that.

'Relax,' he said. He was amused but there was an edge to his voice too. 'I never jumped women in the street even when I was a teenager.'

That, of course, helped a bunch. The thought of Conrad jumping her anywhere, at any age, turned Francesca's bones to water.

'I'm relaxed. I'm relaxed.' It was a mantra. She almost believed it.

She really tried, too. She did all the right things. Asked him in for coffee. Invited him into the kitchen while she was making it, chatting to him as if she had known him all her life. Took the coffee through to the sitting room and curled up on the sofa, kicking off her shoes as if they were total intimates.

Only she didn't meet his eyes. And she kept out of touching distance.

And then Conrad stopped talking. He put down his cup very deliberately. Stood up. Came over to the sofa.

'Francesca.'

She had been talking about a promotion they were thinking

of doing for a local children's author. She skidded to a halt. 'Yes?'

Very gently he leaned forward and swung her legs to the floor. Then he sat down on the sofa beside her.

'We've got to start somewhere.' He sounded horribly calm. She sat like a rabbit in the headlights. 'Er—I suppose so.'

He slid an arm along the back of the seat behind her. 'You're sure your heart isn't broken?'

Well, at least she could answer that one truthfully. 'Absolutely.'

'And there are no other hang-ups I should know about?'

'N-no.'

He looked at her searchingly. 'No unresolved adolescent trauma? No beastly boyfriends with peculiar habits that turned you off anything?'

She swallowed. 'No.'

He smiled. He was so close that it felt as if he was smiling straight into her head. 'No phobias about seismologists? You don't have to worry. We don't bring our own earthquakes, you know.'

That startled her so much that she laughed. Really, truly laughed, without inhibition or embarrassment. Out loud. It was very clever of him.

Because she was laughing when he kissed her.

Oh, yes, very clever. But then, he had had a lot of practice. Even Francesca, foggy with sensation, realised that.

It was in the way he drew her into his arms, firmly but without force. It was in the way he angled her head, so that her face was tilted but there was no strain on her neck. That triggered an unwelcome memory: Barry had always made her feel as if her neck was breaking.

Above all, it was in the way he drew her in to his body, as if they had been doing this forever. As if they were already lovers.

Francesca turned to him like a sunflower to the dawn.

His mouth was gentle. It tantalised. He brushed his lips back and forth across hers, as if they were playing a game. And they both knew the rules.

But I don't, thought Francesca. Or that bit of Francesca that was able to think Most of her was responding to something a lot more basic.

'Why do you always wear glasses?' he murmured. 'Contact lenses would be—friendlier.'

Her mouth felt wonderfully sensual. As if she had suddenly turned into Sheherezade or Madame de Pompadour. She managed, 'The shape of my eyes—'

'Wonderful eyes,' he whispered. 'Toffee-apple eyes.'

She gasped, 'I can't—'

'Yes?' he said encouragingly, stippling tiny kisses along the arch of her throat. 'What can't you do, my beautiful Francesca?'

'I can't—I can't wear contacts. What are you *doing*?' It was a groan.

He did not try to answer. Instead he gave a soft laugh and unhooked her glasses.

Francesca gave up even trying to resist. As she gave a sigh of total surrender her head fell back. She wound her arms round his neck and gave herself up to the sensation of the moment.

And what sensation! He began a leisurely exploration, sliding his hands over every contour, slowly and with pleasure. It was only when she jumped in shock that she realised he had got rid of most of her clothes at the same time.

Her eyes flew open. Wide, myopic eyes that saw breadth of shoulder and a tanned chest under a gaping shirt that she was almost certain she had unbuttoned herself. Feverishly. And— well, that was about it. He was too close. She could not read him. She felt suddenly vulnerable. Cold, too.

Struggling up onto one elbow, she groped for her glasses.

He did not entirely let her go.

'What is it?'

'I can't see you.' She pushed her glasses up her nose.

Just in time to see him smile. The smile was blinding in its triumph.

'Then feel me.'

He took her hand and drew it inside his shirt. She felt his

heart, slow and steady; the texture of this new, stranger's skin; the architecture of ribcage and hip bones…

Its triumph?

Francesca recoiled as if his chest was red-hot and she had scalded her fingers on it.

'What am I doing?' she said, appalled.

Not so long ago she had been lying on this very sofa with Barry de la Touche thinking she was in love with him. And Barry de la Touche had never held her hand to where his heart beat like a sledgehammer and made her feel as if her blood beat to the same rhythm. She looked at Conrad almost in horror.

He did not see it. 'Just going with your instincts,' he drawled against her shoulder.

His breath on her skin made her shiver, deep inside, where no one had ever made her shiver before.

'Please.' She struggled away from him. 'This—isn't me. I don't…'

But the amused, sensual mouth set in a harsh line. No amusement, no sensuality. Just sheer, single-minded determination.

He stopped drifting kisses along her skin. Instead he took her mouth. Hard.

Francesca gave a small squeak. Of shock? Of protest? And then she was drowning.

She wanted to push him away. She told herself she tried to push him away. But really, all she wanted to do was take this journey he had started her on to the very end of the road. She moaned, in exquisite suspension. She felt his hand slide along the smooth flesh of her thigh as if she had been waiting for this touch for all eternity.

Conrad whispered, 'Tell me what you want.'

It shot her out of the spiralling fantasy as if she had been fired from a cannon. She landed back in reality with a shattering thud.

'Stop!' It was almost a scream.

He was as startled as she. His head reared up.

'What is it? What did I do?'

She beat at him with hands as weak as moths. 'I never meant—I never thought—I'm not *like* this Oh, let me go.'

He recoiled as if she had stabbed him. He leaped to his feet. 'What happened?'

Francesca turned her head against the cushion, away from him. 'It's too soon,' she said wearily.

It was nowhere near the whole truth. But it would do for now.

There was an agonising silence. Then little sounds. She realised that he was dressing—buttoning his shirt, putting on his shoes—and she thought, *How could I have let things go this far?*

Above her head he said, 'You want me to go, then?'

Francesca could feel her jaw throbbing with tension. She turned her head against the cushion and looked at him. Oh, he looked so—hurt! *No,* screamed her heart.

'Yes,' said her mouth. And snapped shut like a rat trap.

He took a step back.

But before he went he looked at her for a long moment. She saw herself in his eyes as she lay sprawled among the cushions. Shirt gone. Skirt a crumpled dishcloth under her thighs. Eyes dazed and unfocused, even with her glasses restored to her. Mouth swollen with passion.

More than passion. Need.

Francesca found she did not need glasses to bring the picture into shamefully clear focus.

'Oh, lord,' she said in real horror.

Conrad flinched. And went without a word.

CHAPTER SEVEN

BUT the plan was agreed and he held her to it. Francesca was too proud to back out. She even, at her mother's insistence, took lessons in formal ballroom dancing. I can handle this, she told herself. Though on the night of the hospital ball she stood in front of her bathroom mirror and shook.

She looked like a stranger, she thought. Everything about her was new. New dress, in dramatic, figure-hugging satin. 'It looks like the petticoat from *Cat on a Hot Tin Roof,*' she had protested but Jazz, her style guru, had laughed and told her to be grateful she had the figure for it. New haircut, more aggressively stylish than she had ever had before. New ruby earrings, gift of her father. New make-up, after a make-over day at London's most exclusive salon, gift of her mother.

Even her scent was new. That was a heavily voluptuous mix of spice and herb notes that made her quite giddy. She would not have worn it except that that, too, was a gift. From ex-Queen Angelika.

Conrad's grandmother had been nothing but polite ever since they told her the news together. But she continued to look sceptical, even when Conrad took Francesca's hand and held it. Even when, after Francesca had made everyone laugh for once, he carried it to his lips.

Everyone else thought he adored her. Francesca and his grandmother knew better.

Francesca was not even sure whether the heavy scent was not a subtle insult. It was designed for a woman of mystery, confident in her own sensuality. Not a nit-picking bookseller with a bad crush on unattainable Prince Charming, thought Francesca, castigating herself.

Except, of course, that he was not unattainable. She could

have him on a plate. He had told her as much. But only because she had the right father and had been in the right place at the right time. He had not taken one look at her and fallen desperately in love so that nothing else mattered. She could not have his heart.

And that was what she wanted. The weeks between that night in her apartment and the ball only served to spell it out all too clearly. She wanted Prince Conrad Domitio's heart like she had never wanted anything in her life.

Not an end to her parents' battles. Not to stay in the same school for more than one year at a time. Not to have a father with a lower profile. None of them came anywhere near the intensity with which she wished that Conrad might, one day, fall in love with her. Sometimes she even dreamed that he had, and woke up all softened with love and trust. Only then—

'Oh, yeah? Plain and prickly,' she jeered at her morning reflection. 'Get real.'

So here she was, standing in front of the mirror with gleaming dress, gleaming lips, gleaming nails and rubies in her ears. She should have been everything she had dreamed of being for him. So beautiful he could never call her plain again. Only she did not feel beautiful. And she had a terrible sinking feeling in the pit of her stomach.

The entry phone rang. Ever since that first night Conrad had been meticulous not to surprise her by turning up in the corridor again. She sent one panicky look at her elegant exterior, swallowed hard and buzzed him in.

She stood by the open door of the apartment, drumming her fingers against its white-painted surface, waiting for him. He saw her the moment he got out of the lift. He stopped dead.

'You look—spectacular.'

He did not sound entirely pleased about it. So much for the fantasy! He was not exactly staggering back, gasping with astonishment. Or falling over himself to recall his careless criticism. Francesca would have been disappointed if only she was not already feeling so panicky.

'I look like a complete phoney,' she corrected. Her voice was high and tight as a drum.

'Hey.' He strode forward and took her restless fingers in a steadying clasp. 'What's wrong?'

She let him hold on to her hands. It was comforting.

'Everyone keeps giving me *advice*.'

He chuckled. 'They will do that, won't they? Part of the human condition.'

'They keep telling me how to do things I didn't know I needed to think about. Like curtsey. And get out of a car. And make an entrance into the ballroom,' said Francesca, agitated. 'Mother says, keep my head up. Father says, keep my chin down or I look like a prize fighter. Jazz says, make eye contact with photographers. Your grandmother says, don't look at them. I don't know what to do. I wish I'd never got into this.'

He drew one hand through the crook of his arm. 'Stick with me, kid. I'll get you through.'

She found she believed him. The panic began to evaporate. By the time they arrived at the luxury hotel where the ball was taking place, she was almost calm.

It was just as well. The cameras started the moment she put one high-heeled foot out of the limousine hired for the occasion. Francesca did her best not to wince or to hide her eyes from the popping flashlights. And to remember not to scowl.

'Hang on to me,' Conrad said in her ear. 'I know how to deal with this.'

He put an arm round her and led her up the shallow steps, smiling impartially round at all the cameras.

There was a chorus of 'Look this way, love'; 'Give us a smile'; 'Has he popped the question yet?'; 'Who made your dress?'

He held up his hand for silence. The chorus died down.

'Thank you for your interest in our affairs. But tonight Miss Heller and I are here to support the Montassurran Hospitals Fund. That's the real story. That's what we're really committed to.' He looked down, smiling into her eyes. 'Aren't we, darling?'

The photographers loved it. Well, of course they did. It was the picture they had been trying to get ever since they had caught Francesca, with tears running down her face, running away from the Crown Prince. Francesca found herself leaning into Conrad's embrace as if he was her rock. Well, for the moment, at least, he was. She would have done anything he wanted.

So it was just as well that he turned down the photographers' shouted request for a kiss. He shook his head, smiling.

'Sorry, guys. That comes under the heading of strictly private activity.'

There was a roar of appreciation and at least one ribald suggestion from one of the women. Conrad's arm tightened round Francesca.

He said in her ear, 'One final happy smile all round and we're out of here. Right?'

'Right.'

They didn't quite have to make a break for it. The hotel staff were too well-trained. And besides, another limousine was drawing up behind them. They escaped into the hotel ballroom in good order.

'Well done,' Conrad said. 'No one could have done it better. Stick with me and you're going to make one hell of a princess.'

Francesca laughed. But it was hollow.

She had no time to feel inadequate, however. Almost at once she was curtseying formally to ex-Queen Angelika. She had practised the curtsey but she still had to concentrate. When she rose she saw that the ex-queen was wearing long white gloves. Francesca's Venetian red nails looked brash in contrast.

'Mistake,' she muttered.

But Conrad followed her glance and laughed. 'Your manicure? Forget it. My grandmother will be green with envy. She has bitten her nails as long as I've known her.'

And he swept her off to circulate beside him. Between listening to people who were urgent for Conrad's attention and talking to people she had never met before, she forgot her doubts. And trying to commit names and essential details to memory was too absorbing to allow her any time for feeling phoney. By the time they were seated at the top table, she felt she had been Conrad's girlfriend for half a lifetime.

He was obviously popular, and not just with hot-eyed women who lusted after that lazy, graceful body, as she had feared.

'Such a dear boy,' said a silver-haired woman seated opposite. She leaned forward confidingly. 'So good to see he has got over Silvia at last.'

The man on Francesca's left frowned her down. 'Conrad's a good man,' he said gruffly. 'Excellent paper on longitudinal vibrations. I hear he's talking to the International Architects' Conference in the autumn.'

'Who is Silvia?' said Francesca.

'Great honour for a non-architect to be asked,' said her neighbour, sticking to his point valiantly.

She looked at the silver-haired woman. 'Silvia?'

The woman sighed. 'Oh, my dear. I suppose they don't talk about her. That was what the family always called his wife. Ex-wife now, of course. Princess Marie Elena. But his mother was Elena, and after she and his father were killed nobody wanted to think about that. So they always called her Silvia.'

Francesca sat very, very still. She felt all the lovely, careless confidence she had not even known she had garnered begin to leak away as if someone had pulled the plug. Leaving her empty.

'Oh,' she said, after what seemed to her hours. 'His wife. Of course.'

'Ex-wife,' corrected her neighbour swiftly.

'Ex-wife, of course.'

How could she not have known? How could no one have told her? Not her father. Not her mother.

Above all, how could Conrad not have told her? When he'd said, 'Let's do it for real,' why had he not said at the same time, 'After all, I've done it before'? She felt as if the ice were closing round her, over her, pressing her down.

She sat through the speeches, the appeals, feeling numb. When Felix declared that it was time for dancing, she clapped like the rest, her mouth stiff with smiling.

Conrad came over at once. He held his hand out, smiling. His eyes were green.

Oh, he was so sure of her, thought Francesca. A little crack appeared in the ice. When she thawed she was going to be furious, she knew. Maybe it would be as well if she did not thaw until they were out of here, somewhere decently private. Where she could throw things.

He took her into his arms and swung her onto the floor for the old-fashioned waltz that opened the dancing. He must have felt the tension in her spine.

'What's wrong?' he murmured into her hair.

'Nothing.' She kept smiling firmly over his shoulder.

'No one has said anything to upset you?'

Upset? Heavens!

'No.'

'No one has said anything nasty about your father?'

Both her parents were here tonight, setting aside their estrangement for the occasion. Her father's name featured prominently on the list of benefactors thanked in the glossy ball programme. But Francesca knew that the old-guard Montassurran nobility were not anything like as grateful as the hospitals-ball committee would like everyone to think.

'No one's mentioned Dad.'

He gave a sigh of relief.

'Well, then. Let's kick back and have fun.'

Francesca wanted to kill him.

'Let's,' she agreed between gritted teeth.

Her parents watched the circling couple with varying degrees of satisfaction.

Lady Anne was looking startlingly glamorous. She was wearing black velvet and a diamond choker that Peter had given her when he finalised his first big deal. She came over to him, for the first time since they had arrived together.

'Well, it worked. You owe me, you know.'

'Thank you,' said Peter stiffly.

His ex-wife looked at him with a good deal of comprehension. He would so much rather have organised everything himself, she thought fondly. But you could never afford to let Peter see that he amused you. It made him wild with fury.

So, 'I didn't do it for you,' she said in her cool, indifferent voice. 'I did it for my daughter.'

In spite of the fact that it was what he wanted himself, he could not resist a little taunt. 'Because he's a prince? You are such a snob!'

'Because he made her cry,' said Lady Anne serenely.

Peter was genuinely horrified. He turned burning eyes on her. 'What kind of mother are you? You want a man to make our daughter cry?'

Francesca and Conrad had reached a massively swathed heraldic shield and paused to let a small bottleneck of dancers disentangle itself. Peter took an impetuous step in their direction. He found his arm taken in a strong grip.

'Leave them alone.'

'But—*cry*!' He was revolted.

'Oh, you are so stupid about people.' She was exasperated. 'Think. Nobody makes Francesca cry. We certainly didn't. Those terrible girls at all those schools didn't. Not even when they laughed at her. Even Barry de la Touche didn't, as far as I can tell.'

'Trott,' said Peter automatically.

Lady Anne made an impatient gesture. 'Whatever. She was going to marry him, you know. Before you went steaming in and got her dumped in public.'

He stuck his chin out, looking mulish. 'There was no engagement.'

She sighed. 'He'd asked her. She was thinking about it. She told me he made her feel beautiful. But then you got rid of him. And she didn't shed a tear. But Conrad Domitio made her cry and we've got the pictures to prove it.'

Peter's chin came down. 'I see what you mean,' he said slowly.

'I doubt it.' She was acid. 'But, like I said, you owe me a favour.'

He was bridling at once. 'What do you want?'

'Leave them alone.'

'What?'

'You've done enough meddling in Francesca's life. Now leave her to get on with it. She and Conrad can work it out on their own.'

'But—'

'Or not. Maybe they won't get it together. Either way, it's not our business. Right?'

Peter looked arrested. '*Our* business,' he echoed.

For the first time she looked uncertain. 'What?'

'Dance with me,' he said.

He slid an arm round her and led her out onto the dance floor before she had time to think of an answer.

Francesca said chattily, 'When were you going to tell me about your wife?'

Conrad's ballroom hold was suddenly a vice. 'What are you talking about?'

'Silvia. Isn't that her name? When were you going to bring her into the equation?'

'Oh, Silvia.'

He sounded impatient. How dared he sound impatient?

'Your wife. Yes?'

'Ex-wife.'

'Gosh, you've got a lot of exes in your family,' she said. 'Ex-king. Ex-queen. Ex-wife. Not good at holding on to things, are you?'

Conrad looked confused. 'That's not kind.'

'No,' agreed Francesca raging. She followed him in the

steps of an expert reverse—thank you, Mother—and gave him a bright, furious smile.

'And not like you.'

'Oh, but it is. I'm the one who likes to get my facts straight, remember. So straighten me out on Silvia. When? Where? Why? And how long?'

He looked round, harassed out of his habitual cool. 'We can't talk about it here.'

'Then let's go somewhere we *can* talk about it,' she flung at him.

'All right, then.'

'All right.'

They exchanged looks like duellists. Then Conrad gave an odd little ceremonious bow and led her off the floor.

Everyone in the room watched them. A fair proportion sighed sentimentally.

He took her out of the ballroom, down the stairs and out into the street. It was the back entrance of the hotel. A sleepy commissionaire asked if they wanted a taxi.

'No,' said Conrad curtly.

He took her hand and ran with her, down the hill and across a road to a slate wall. The Thames was a gorge of glittering stars and reflected light.

Francesca looked down into the black, shifting water. She felt as if she were on the edge of a precipice. She swung round, her bare shoulders gleaming in the street lights.

'Tell me the truth, Conrad.'

He turned and leaned on the river wall. His hair stirred in the faint spring breeze. He seemed unaware of it. The scent of his cologne flicked at her, elusive as the breeze, then was gone.

He said wearily, 'I thought everyone knew.'

'Not me.'

'Why not? You knew everything else. Even the Congress of Vienna.' He pulled himself together and went on quietly, 'We were both very young. It was—a suitable match, I suppose you might say.'

Francesca winced, unseen. She restrained herself from saying 'That's more than I am',

'Her father was Felix's minister of home affairs in exile. We had the same great-great-great-grandmother. She knew what was expected.'

He sounded so bleak that, against all her expectations, Francesca felt a sneaking sympathy for him.

'Why did you marry her?'' she asked gruffly.

'I was crown prince, all of a sudden. My parents had been drowned—oh, yes, you know about that, don't you? I was still in college. But suddenly I had no home. Oh, Felix and Angelika were brilliant. But they run something between a court and a refugee centre. It's not a family home. I was twenty. Felix started talking about heirs. I thought—children will make a home again.' He looked across the river, his profile harsh. 'I was stupid. But at twenty you see what you want to see.'

She was shaken. This was worse than she had dreamed of. 'Children?'

'Oh, don't worry. Silvia didn't want children. Not for years, at least. She was rather good on the neuroses that made me want them,' he said savagely. Then stopped abruptly, pushing a hand through his hair. 'Oh, what's the use? She was probably right. I wasn't old enough to be a father. And I was a terrible prig, too.'

Francesca could not imagine the man who had driven her to the edge of ecstasy ever being a prig. She judged that now was not the right time to say so.

'So what happened?'

He narrowed his eyes at the National Theatre, on the other side of the river, as if it were a personal enemy.

He said in a hard voice, 'She did what all unhappy wives do. She found herself another man.'

Francesca moved close enough to touch his shoulder. And when he seized her hand, almost crunching the bones of her fingers, she did not utter a single protest.

Conrad did not look at her. He told the river, 'I'm a good

lover. Sometimes I can be a really great lover. But I'm a terrible husband.'

She held her breath.

He turned, not leaving go of her hand but not otherwise touching her.

He said raggedly, 'Marry me! Marry me *now*!'

Hell, thought Conrad. This wasn't how it was supposed to be. This wasn't how he had planned it at all.

He had known exactly where he was going to take her. His grandparents had taken a suite in the hotel for the night. The suite had a quietly luxurious sitting room. He had filled it with flowers. A bottle of champagne awaited. Along with the heirloom ring which he had already had altered to fit Francesca's small hand.

He had promised her a real wooing. And a good old-fashioned formal proposal was part of that. When she looked back on the time he asked her to marry him he had wanted her to be able to remember more than a grubby coffee bar full of tourists and herself saying, 'Are you out of your mind?' Only—he had wanted her to remember music and flowers and candlelight. Not this.

Not with her hurt and angry, shivering beside him in the night air. Not with her nipples hardening under that damn heart-attack of a dress, only from cold, not from what he was doing to her. Not with him sounding—well, desperate.

Conrad straightened, pulling himself together with an effort. He wanted to hold her so much, it was a physical pain. And it would be the worst mistake he could make. He let go of her hands.

'I'm sorry,' he said quietly. 'Forget I said that.'

Francesca gave him one of her bright smiles. He was learning to dread them.

'Oh, I don't know. It was memorable.'

'Francesca—'

'That's what you wanted, wasn't it? That's what this real wooing of yours was supposed to do, wasn't it? Give me something to remember?'

He could see that she was angry. He did not know why.

'Yes, but—I hoped you would enjoy yourself tonight. What's wrong with that?'

'Wooing,' said Francesca between chattering teeth, 'is about more than enjoying yourself.'

Conrad would have taken issue with that. But he was concerned. She was starting to shake.

'You're cold,' he said remorsefully. 'I should never have brought you out here.'

He shrugged off his black jacket and swung it round her. She jumped and made a small noise of distress.

Oh, no, thought Conrad wearily, what else can go wrong?

'Come on,' he said levelly. 'Let's get you inside.'

But, 'No,' she said, hanging on to his arm. 'I'll be all right. Let's walk. This is important.'

He stared down at her, trying to make out her expression. But in the strange glare of the north-bank streetlights he saw only the compressed line of her mouth. He could feel the persistent tremors running through her, though. Of course, both could be due to cold as much as anger. Or—he winced at the thought—hurt.

He put an arm round her body, pulling her against him.

'OK. We'll walk a while. If that's what you want. But the moment your feet turn to ice we're indoors. Right?'

'Right.' She gave a shaky laugh and pulled the edges of his jacket together at her throat.

The two-lane highway was almost deserted. There was no one else on the pavement. An occasional car flashed by, all lemon headlights and the sound of speed, and disappeared at the curve of the river. When it had gone their footsteps were left clipping the paving like the start of an old-fashioned horror movie. In the distance the clock tower of Big Ben and the gothic buttresses of the Houses of Parliament stood out against a black velvet sky.

Francesca was not looking at Big Ben. She had her head down.

She said into his jacket, 'So tell me why your marriage broke up.'

'I told you—'

She looked up then, her eyes flashing. Or maybe that was the effect of the sodium streetlights on her glasses.

'It can't have been just because you were a prig who wanted children.'

'Oh, that precise mind,' he said, between annoyance and concern.

He had a sudden suspicion that she was on the edge of tears. His arm tightened round her. He could not bear to think of his Francesca crying. She was such a fighter. It would not be fair.

He said honestly, 'No, it was a lot more than that. But basically it was because we were both too young and I didn't understand what she wanted.'

Francesca stopped. Perforce he stopped too.

'What she wanted?' she echoed.

'To be a princess,' he said evenly. 'She wanted to go to Ascot and Monaco and opening nights at the Met. She wanted a designer wardrobe and a jet-set lifestyle. She wanted to be a celebrity. She didn't want to be married to a working seismologist whose only travel plans were to earthquake hotspots.' He stopped. 'She didn't want *me*,' he finished in a low voice.

Her eyes were huge behind her glasses.

'But didn't you tell her—?'

'No. No, I didn't tell her anything. I didn't think I needed to. Her family had known mine all my life. I thought she knew what it would be like.'

Even to himself he sounded unbearably weary. He had thought all this was over. Why on earth was he sounding as if he was still hurt by it? What was the point of digging up those old disappointments now?

She scanned his face. 'You said you were a bad husband but a—a—' she boggled at the phrase and his arm tightened involuntarily '—a good lover. Is that why she left you?'

'You mean, did I screw around? No.' He paused, then added honestly, 'She said I was more married to my job than I was to her. I admit I was very tied up with it. I'd get involved up at the lab and forget we were going out to dinner, that sort of thing. She said I'd rather talk to other seismologists than to her.'

Francesca digested this. 'Was she right?' she said at last.

He felt a little spurt of irritation. He had promised himself he would never dig around in this miserable stuff again. He had fought so hard to keep his marriage on the road but he had started to fight too late. 'What is this, the inquisition?'

'Was she *right?*'

He gave an exasperated sigh. 'Hell, yes, she was right. I told you—I was too young to get married.'

'So why did you?' Still that little, emotionless voice, like a very young prosecuting attorney. Or a judge.

His brows twitched together. A judge! Hell and damnation! He did not answer.

'You were in love with her, weren't you?'

'I—'

'You were young. You'd lost your parents. And the hormones were on full alert.'

She was distant as the moon. He had his arm round her, holding her so tight that he could feel every breath she took. But even so he felt he could not reach her. Was never going to reach her again. And the distance had nothing to do with physical configuration.

She said in that silvery voice, 'Of course you were in love with her.'

And lying between them, heavy as lead, was the thing she did not say: *And you're not in love with me.*

His heart twisted in his breast. Somehow he had managed to hurt this woman badly.

'Oh, Francesca,' he said involuntarily.

'It's all right. I just wanted to know.' But she drew away from the shelter of his arm. 'I think I'd like to go in now. We've got an engagement to announce.'

Conrad was appalled at what he had done. 'No,' he said violently. 'Not if you're unhappy.'

She turned a blind face to him. This time the smile was a grimace.

'Oh, no,' she said politely. 'Why should I be unhappy? I'm doing my bit for Montassurro. And flashing my engagement ring all over the tabloids at the same time. Any girl would be proud.'

He was shocked. What have I done? he thought. What have I done to her?

'We don't have to announce anything tonight. We're not committed.'

She clutched the jacket round her. 'Yes, we do,' she said obstinately. 'It will put the Montassurran Hospitals Fund on every front page in the country. Let's get it over with.' She shivered convulsively. *'Please.'*

What could he do? He took her back to the ballroom.

Francesca felt as if she was in a nightmare. The lining of his jacket felt unbearably erotic against the bare skin of her shoulders. It reminded her of his skin against hers when they had lain together on her sofa. She remembered the feel of his bones under her fingers and the smell of his hair.

Had she thought he might come to love her? Had she really thought that? What a pathetic person she was!

This was a classic marriage of convenience. It had been spelled out for her in letters a foot high, right from the start. Why, she'd even initiated the first approach herself, telling her father that she wanted to meet Prince Conrad Domitio.

Oh, she'd contributed to her own downfall, all right. She couldn't blame anyone but herself. A few meetings, a couple of dozen teasing phone calls, and she had fallen as completely in love as it was possible to be.

She could not blame Conrad. He had told the truth, from the moment he knew who she was. He had never tried to pretend he was in love with her. He didn't want to break her heart. Even now, the man was trying to let her off the hook.

So why hadn't she grabbed the opportunity and run like mad?

Her whole body hurt with the answer.

Because I'm in love with him. And I'm stupid enough to think that if I hang on in there he might one day come to love me.

Yeah. Right. Sure. Likely, or what?

Because I'm in love with him and he needs me.

She could still hear that ragged voice in her head. 'Marry me!' Not the proposal of a man bent on giving her the wooing experience of the century. Rather, a man on the edge, reaching out.

So there was her answer. He needed her.

'This,' she told herself grimly in the mirror of the sumptuous ladies', 'is ridiculous. Patient Griselda, you're not.'

But she held the collar of his jacket to her nostrils and inhaled the scent of him, like the bouquet of a fine wine. She'd never done that to any of Barry's clothes. Or any of the other men she'd dated. This one was special. This one seemed to be fate.

'As long as he's straight with me,' said Francesca, giving fate a chance. 'If he starts telling me lies to be kind, I'm outta here.'

The engagement ring was a big square-cut ruby surrounded by diamonds. It looked almost too big for Francesca's small finger. On the other hand, it looked brilliant against the gleaming stuff of her dress. And the pendant earrings, extravagant gift of Peter Heller, had clearly been designed to match it exactly.

The reporters were ecstatic. The royal family was ecstatic. Courtiers who had known Crown Prince Conrad since he was a baby were ecstatic. There was so much off-the-record briefing going on round the ballroom that the dance floor thinned out noticeably.

Francesca smiled until her teeth ached. Conrad, his jacket restored to him, never left her side. He parried a lot of the questions but of course there were many she had to answer herself.

Yes, she was over the moon. Yes, he had made her a romantic proposal. Yes, she was wildly in love. No, they hadn't set a date for the wedding yet, but it wouldn't be this year. They both had commitments.

And then his grandmother cornered her. Her white gloves were still immaculate and her eyes were still cool. Not exactly hostile, just neutral, waiting. As far as ex-Queen Angelika was concerned, thought Francesca, the jury was out on her grandson's chosen bride.

'Are you going with him to Montassurro?' the ex-queen asked, without preamble.

Francesca was startled. 'Well, yes, of course. Eventually, I suppose.'

'I mean, when he takes the mobile hospital over.'

'We hadn't discussed it…'

'Discuss it,' the ex-queen advised.

Francesca shifted uncomfortably. 'Thank you for your advice but—'

'Conrad is like his grandfather. He's honest, intelligent, hard-working and a dream to go to bed with.'

Francesca gasped and went faintly pink.

The ex-queen sighed. 'I thought your generation was supposed to be so uninhibited. Anyway, so I'm told. But if he has a fault it is that he is single-minded. That's what Silvia couldn't understand. She let him go off chasing earthquakes, never realising that meant he forgot all about her for months at a time.'

'You think he'll forget me while he's in Montassurro.'

'I think he'll have a damn good try. Conrad is not comfortable with intimacy. Never was, even as a child.'

Francesca thought of the warmth of his jacket around her shoulders. Of that ragged, 'Marry me!' She looked at where he was standing, his back to her, head bent, listening to the businessmen. As if he felt her eyes on him, he looked round and smiled. Her mouth curved involuntarily. Conrad didn't do intimacy, did he?

'No?'

Conrad's grandmother raised her eyebrows. 'Maybe he's changed.' She sounded sceptical. 'I'd still go with him.'

'Would you? Why?'

'The first weeks after an engagement are critical. That's when both parties get cold feet. Besides,' the narrowed, neutral eyes were alarmingly perceptive, 'don't you *want* to go with him? Tall, dark and handsome and he's all yours. Don't you want to see what happens?'

She gave a regal nod and left.

She left Francesca speechless. Conrad saw it when he returned to her side.

'What is it?' he said in quick concern.

'Your grandmother—'

He followed the direction of her gaze. 'What has she done now?' he said in quick concern.

'She more or less told me to get you into bed quickly before you got away.' Francesca was outraged.

But she was unsettled too. Since that evening in her flat Conrad had chivalrously kept his hands off her. Now—well, she did not want him to keep his hands off any more. She was going to have to let him know that.

It was not easy when he was roaring with laughter.

'You must have misunderstood,' he said, when he could speak. 'My grandmother is a fully paid-up member of the virginity-before-marriage brigade.'

'No, she isn't. She was telling me to come to Montassurro with you and—'

'Make love every step of the way?' teased Conrad.

'Yes. I...'

And then she realised what the ex-queen was saying. If she believed in virginity before marriage, that was. Sleep with him but don't marry him! Don't spoil my grandson's life!

And I wanted him to love me!

All the lovely, golden confidence disappeared in a second. Embarrassment caught up with her. Crippling, cruel embarrassment. If his grandmother had deliberately set out to ensure that they did not spend the night together she could not have been more effective. Francesca felt her limbs turn to lead.

She gave him a strained smile. 'I'm sorry. I'm very tired all of a sudden. How long before we—I mean, I can go home?'

'*We*,' he said emphatically, 'can leave whenever you like.'

'You don't have to take me home.'

He took her hands. 'Yes, I do,' he said quietly.

And the sexual question was there between them. Two hours ago—hell, two minutes ago—she would have fallen into his arms and counted all her dreams fulfilled. But his grandmother had finished that.

Her message had been so clear. Conrad will take you to bed and you will have a wonderful time. But he won't let you get close. And he won't love you.

It was what he had said himself. Great lover. Terrible husband.

And I want him for a husband, thought Francesca, a real husband who loves and wants me.

She tried to say something, to tell him how she felt. Or hide how she felt and ask him to make love to her anyway. She couldn't.

Conrad saw her withdrawal at once, of course. 'Relax,' he said wearily, letting go of her hands. 'You aren't going to have to fight me off. I'll take you home and leave you.'

'I—'

'That's what you want, isn't it?' he demanded harshly.

She wished it wasn't. How she wished it wasn't. Almost, for a moment, she talked herself back into wanting to go to bed with him again. But he was standing there, all gorgeously rumpled, with a faint shadow of beard appearing, and he had never felt more alien. More—Francesca said it to herself deliberately—out of her league.

'Yes,' she said desolately.

'Then let's go.'

He left her at the door to her apartment. He did not even kiss her. And when he had gone she had her first ever night without any sleep at all.

I've got to do something about this, she thought, sitting gritty-eyed and wretched in her kitchen at five-thirty in the morning. How am I going to tell him I made a mistake? He looked so hurt!

That was when she remembered the rest of his grand-mother's message. Maybe there was something in that advice.

That morning, as soon as she decently could, she called Conrad's number in Cambridge and left a message. She had rehearsed it and rehearsed it until she was word-perfect. It was jokey, no pressure, and it meant the world to her.

'The first time we met you said you could use a precision merchant like me on your team. Well, here's your chance. I want to come with you to Montassurro.'

CHAPTER EIGHT

THEY set off six weeks later. The trust had managed to fit up three first-aid buses to deliver basic hygiene and emergency treatment, and a full-scale mobile hospital. Francesca did not have a licence to drive any of them. Not at all to her surprise, Conrad did.

'You're bound to be an inspired map-reader,' he said to Francesca with that charming, slightly cool manner he had used to her since the ball.

It was perfectly friendly, but it kept her at a distance. Of course, she could not expect him to be all over her in the middle of a sizeable party like this. But she would have been grateful for the odd touch. Even a smile that said they were close would have been welcome. But he treated her exactly the same as he treated everyone else in his team.

'Don't worry,' Jazz told her comfortingly, helping her pack. 'He's protecting you really. The Press are still after you. You don't want pictures of the two of you in the clinch of the year all over the tabloids, do you?'

'Do you think that's what it is?' said Francesca. She was doubtful. 'It doesn't feel like being protected. It feels as if he's pushing me away.'

'Have a heart! The guy's got a convoy to get across half a continent. Then up some of the most horrible roads in Europe. He's probably got a lot of his mind on that.'

Francesca bit her lip. 'Yes, of course.'

'Just slipstream behind him for the moment,' advised Jazz. 'Let him deliver the hospital stuff. Then he can afford the time to do the full Casanova afterwards.'

'Yes,' said Francesca. But she was unconvinced.

In fact, she was losing conviction by the day. If Jazz had

149

not thrown herself so wholeheartedly into the preparations she might even have backed out. But Jazz had found a budding novelist to cover for Francesca in the shop while she was away. Besides, Conrad had warned everyone to travel light and Francesca had sought advice from Jazz, an experienced backpacker. As a result, her bag was a miracle of space-saving ingenuity.

'All temperatures, all weathers, any type of social engagement,' said Jazz with relish. 'Rule one: wash whatever you can whenever you get the chance.'

'Wash,' said Francesca, committing it to memory.

'Never add anything to the bag unless you've managed to get rid of something first.'

'No new additions.'

'And never go anywhere without baby wipes.'

'What?'

'Well, once you're there, you'll be doing the princess-elect thing, right? Lots of receiving bouquets and hugging babies? Well, let me tell you, not all bouquets come in silver-lined boxes and Cellophane. If the flowers have just been hauled off the bush you'll get green stuff on your hands. And that's nothing to what small children do. Think of your average four-year-old,' said Jazz, who had brothers, sisters and nephews by the bus-load, 'as a walking pot of yoghurt that is past its sell-by date. And leaks. Baby wipes get you through.'

Jazz was not the only one who contributed. Lady Anne gave her a long black dress that folded up into nothing.

'It will do anything, even a formal dinner if it has to. Find some local costume jewellery to dress it up when you're there,' she advised practically. 'That way you're supporting the local economy and looking as if you've made an effort as well. Good luck.'

She sounded as if she thought Francesca would need it.

Peter Heller gave her a Swiss Army knife and a list of useful contacts. 'Just for emergencies.'

Ex-King Felix gave her a Montassurran phrase book and his

blessing. It sounded as if it choked him. His wife gave her some advice.

'Just because you are going on this boy-scout expedition, you cannot afford to behave like a nobody,' she told Francesca. 'The eyes of the world will be on you.'

'Well, your eyes anyway,' agreed Francesca. She was tired of the older woman's hostility.

'Of course. Conrad is my grandson. I want him to be happy.'

Francesca fired up at that. 'Do you think I don't?'

Ex-Queen Angelika pursed her lips. 'We'll see.'

But when Francesca had left the ex-queen permitted herself a thoroughly unregal grin. Not that anyone else saw it, not even Felix.

So Francesca joined the convoy.

And Conrad treated her as one of the boys.

All across Europe, she saw him as she had never seen him before. Tyres burst and he organised replacements. A driver and navigator came to blows and he negotiated a truce.

Then they got into Montassurro; and it was even worse. Roads were blocked and he found his way round them. The wild, beautiful landscape did not quite match their map; Conrad tramped over the fields to find a local guide. And all the time he was steady as a rock—competent, resourceful, diplomatic and very, very calm.

Francesca began to see what she had previously only suspected—that Conrad was a very serious person indeed. Her heart glowed with pride.

But at the same time her head said to her, Feeling inadequate yet? Why should a man who is this good at anything he turns his hand to bother about a woman who has never held down a job for more than six months?

The answer was clear, of course. She was the daughter of the richest man ever to be born in Montassurro. Her father's list of contacts burned a hole in her pocket.

Meanwhile she followed Jazz's advice to the letter and even got a brief word of praise from Conrad.

'I knew you'd be an asset,' he said as they prepared to have dinner on wooden tables outside a village taverna in the mountains one night.

'Wow,' said Francesca. 'An asset. There's a real compliment.'

His eyes glinted appreciatively. 'You have no idea how right you are.'

'Right *and* an asset! I'll get a swollen head,' she said drily.

He touched her cheek. It was the first time he had laid a hand on her since the night of the ball. 'Not you.' It was very soft, as if it was for her ears alone.

Francesca stood totally still.

But he was called to give a decision by two men poring over the map.

She shook her head and went and sat against the wall of the single-storey building. Face it, she told herself. The man is the leader of a complicated expedition. His directions are needed everywhere. We'll be communicating in snatched half-sentences until we deliver these trucks. There's no time for anything else until the expedition is over. Anyway, he thinks you're an asset!

She tipped her head back, looking up at the stars. They were brilliant and dazzlingly close in the high mountain air. It would have been nice if Conrad had been there to look at them with her.

Even nicer if he thought she emitted some of that stardust! Asset was good. Having him acknowledge that sometimes she was right was good. But Francesca could not help wishing that she dazzled him. Just a little!

Get real, she told herself. You're the girl with the key to a public profile and a lot of rich benefactors. He likes you. Even values you. That's a lot more than most people have.

But I want him to love me.

In your dreams.

Francesca got to her feet and made herself therapeutically busy until she was so tired she was falling over in her tracks.

In the end they got to the biggest town in the mountains for which the hospital truck was destined. It was not much more than a big village with a mediaeval market square and a cluster of houses around it. Two local doctors came to meet them and more or less brushed the delivery team out of the way, so eager were they to get at the new equipment.

'The engine was hardly cool before they were operating on a boy with appendicitis,' wrote Conrad in his journal.

He was seated under an awning at one of the square's three boulevard cafés. Francesca read it over his shoulder.

'Do you always keep a diary?' she asked, sitting down.

He looked up. 'No. Only on expeditions.' He closed the book and pushed it away. 'Originally it was a useful guide to the order in which things happened. You don't always remember in strict sequence. Then I started putting in my own reflections. Just a few of them, to amuse myself.'

He leaned back in the peeling chair. He looked lazy, tanned and incredibly attractive.

Francesca reminded herself that she was not going to let herself be distracted until the journey was over. She rearranged her voice into polite-enquiry mode. 'Is that what the volcano book was?'

He smiled. 'I just supplied the decorative text to frame the photographs. But yes, it all came out of my diary.'

She nodded. 'And when you said you did it for the money…?'

He looked at the hospital truck across the square. 'The advance bought a bit of the portable X-ray machine in there. It remains to be seen what the royalties can afford.'

'They all go direct to the Hospital Fund? I see.'

He shook his head. 'I'm really not interested in money. You got that wrong. I never was. I like doing things.'

Francesca digested this. 'Yes, I can see that. But for Montassurro—'

'I would do a lot for my country,' he said quietly. 'I wouldn't put myself up for auction.'

Francesca remembered: he had said to his grandmother, 'I'm not into human sacrifice.'

Maybe he wanted her for more than her inheritance and her contacts, after all. Yet—how on earth would she ever know? She searched his face. He met her eyes calmly.

'Wouldn't you? But what about your grandfather's election bid?' She worried at her lower lip. 'You'd do a lot for your grandfather, wouldn't you?'

He leaned across the table and put a finger on her mouth. 'Why do you do that? You'll make it sore.'

Francesca jumped. Her pulse shot through the roof and then settled back somewhere in the two-beats-a-minute field. She felt turned to stone.

He ran his thumb along her lower lip. It was slow and strange and infinitely sensuous. She was hardly aware of it when her lips parted.

Conrad's eyes changed; became intent. He bent towards her, his breath quickening.

And there was a shout from the square.

'Damn,' he said with real fury.

A convoy came round the corner. Men in suits. Cameras. A man walking backwards with a big fuzzy sausage on the end of a robot arm, held just above the party's heads.

'Television,' said Conrad wearily. 'I wondered how long it would take the politicians to get in on the act.' He stood up, his eyes on the advancing gaggle.

Francesca watched him. She was beyond putting a guard on her expression. If he looked at her he would see her heart in her eyes, she thought. It would all be there—her bewilderment, her longing, her wild hope and her total disbelief. She felt naked.

'Sorry, I'm going to have to...' He looked back at her. And stopped dead. 'Francesca!'

She was startled. 'What?'

'Don't look at me like that.' His voice was ragged.

He came round the café table so that his body masked her from the street. He did not kiss her. But he cupped her jaw briefly, tenderly. Then he touched her chin; finally her lips, like some sort of tender ritual. She pressed her lips to the back of his hand in a fleeting kiss.

Fleeting but real. They both knew it. He groaned.

'Hold that thought,' he told her on a breathless laugh.

And went to meet his public.

The new arrivals had flown in by helicopter with a substantial entourage. The politicians made speeches, but it was Crown Prince Conrad that the media was interested in. They crowded round with questions and comments and requests—and then, inevitably, they wanted to see Francesca.

That was when what she afterwards thought of as the circus started.

Politicians embraced her. Officials asked her advice. Local worthies solicited her patronage for charitable foundations. Mothers thrust babies into her arms. Small girls curtsied and gave her bouquets. It went on for days.

From being a workmanlike asset to the team, she turned into a fairy off the Christmas tree, as she said privately to Conrad. It made her uneasy.

'Jazz said it would be all babies and bouquets,' she said gloomily. 'I didn't believe her. But she was right, wasn't she?'

'You're doing fine,' he told her, laughing.

'But I would so much rather be up in the villages with you in the first-aid bus.'

'Would you?' He was surprised.

They were walking along outside the mediaeval walls at sunset. All day the heat had pushed at them like a rough young animal. Francesca had taken refuge in shadowed buildings when she could, but Conrad had been out in the hills with the first-aid team. It was milder now, but even so the dust that spurted from under Francesca's sandalled feet was diamond-dry and hot.

Above their heads, the mountain peaks reared like monsters' teeth. Clouds swirled round their summits. It did not look cool even up there.

They were alone for the first time in days and only because Conrad had struck a deal with the Press.

'We'll have to go to a major reception in Vilnagrad,' he told Francesca, pausing to look at the spectacular view. 'I've promised them a full question-and-answer session then. All the photographs they want. So they'll leave us alone for the next two days while we deliver the last first-aid bus.'

She did not like the sound of that. 'That would be a major Press conference?' she asked in trepidation.

He hugged her. 'Don't worry about it.'

'I know,' she said with amused resignation. 'Stick with you and you'll see me through. Right?'

He kissed the top of her head. 'Always.'

She felt warm right down to her toes. 'Conrad, are you sure?'

'If I can handle Felix, I can handle a bunch of hacks,' he said carelessly.

Francesca believed him.

'It's nice to be in the hands of an expert,' she murmured mischievously.

His arm tightened alarmingly. 'You'd better believe it.'

She let her head fall onto his shoulder. But she murmured, 'Careful. You may have negotiated a ceasefire with the hacks. But there's a child climbing up that slope. Any moment now it is going to come bursting out of the undergrowth with a bouquet or an autograph book.'

Conrad stopped and looked down at her. 'Curse all children,' he said roughly.

He kissed her hard. Francesca gave a sigh of blissful surrender.

The sun dipped below the horizon, sending long triangular beams of burning apricot stabbing into the shadowed forest and turning the walled town to gold.

The child arrived, as forecast. It was about eight, of indeterminate sex. It slid out from under a tangle of climbing weeds and surveyed them. It was holding a cheap camera suggestively.

Conrad raised his head reluctantly and snapped something in Montassurran. The child shrugged and stood its ground.

'What did you say?' asked Francesca, amused.

'Shouldn't you be in bed?' translated Conrad.

But the urchin could speak English, it seemed. 'Wanna picture? I make you very good price,' it said briskly.

For a moment Francesca thought Conrad was going to explode. Then he sat down on a fallen boulder, dropped his head in his hands and laughed until he cried.

Francesca could not resist. 'Take a photograph of him now,' she encouraged the urchin. 'I'll buy the whole film.'

In the end the child used up the roll of film on the crown prince chasing his beloved with a fistful of weeds which he stuffed down the back of her T-shirt. That was just before he kissed her so enthusiastically that her feet left the rock-strewn ground.

'Bring me the pictures tomorrow,' Francesca instructed the child, weak with laughter. 'At the Taverna San Simeone. They'll be worth every penny.'

But the child was late. And the first-aid bus left early. So she did not take delivery of the pictures before they left for their last delivery.

The clouds round last night's peaks had been an ominous sign, although they had not realised it. The thunderstorm broke before they were halfway to the high village. Rain hit the potholed road with the force of tsunami.

Francesca was in the accompanying four-wheel drive. They had fallen behind to leave the labouring bus room to manoeuvre. There must have been a quarter of a mile between them when they saw the bus start to aquaplane.

Sitting next to the driver of the Jeep, Francesca was the first to see what was happening. She screamed. She could not help herself. She saw Conrad fighting with the great wheel as the bus slid and bucked, like a ship on a stormy ocean.

Her driver slammed on his brakes. They sat there watching, helpless.

'God, he can drive,' muttered her chauffeur.

He was a local and he spoke in Montassurran but, after days on the road studying the phrase book Felix had given her,

Francesca could understand him easily. Even if her vocabulary had not already been wide enough, the wholehearted admiration in his voice would have told her what he meant.

She tried to feel proud—and confident in Conrad's ability to get them out of danger—but all she felt was a desperate urge to be with him. She folded her hands together to stop them trembling and told herself that he could take care of himself. All she would do was distract his attention if she started falling apart. But she had to press her teeth together so hard to stop herself from crying out that she could feel the vibration in her ears.

The bus had come to rest dangerously close to the precipice. As soon as it stopped rocking Francesca whipped out of the Jeep and ran up the slope. She was almost certain that at least one of the bus's wheels was over the edge.

Pebbles were beginning to rattle down the mountainside, dislodged by the downpour. The rain fell in a grey sheet, stabbed through with dagger flashes of lightning. It would not be long before rocks followed the pebbles, Francesca thought. Her palms were wet with fear.

The offside door of the bus opened. The doctor, nurse and the local official who had been travelling with Conrad eased carefully down onto the road. Then joined Francesca.

'He's going to try to jump it back onto the road,' reported the doctor. 'We're going to try to rig up some anchor ropes, as a safety precaution. What have you got in the back?'

Fortunately there were several industrial-strength pieces of rope. They all worked fast, securing the bus to various ancient trees, leaving just enough play for the ropes to pull taut when the bus moved. The doctor attached the longest rope to an outcrop of rock, just round the bend. Francesca padded the rock wall with the new seat cushions from the bus, to stop the rock sawing into the rope. They gathered by the front of the bus again.

'What about a tow line to the Jeep?' the doctor called up.

'Too dangerous,' said Conrad. 'The bus is heavy enough to pull that off the road too.'

'But it could stabilise you. Those four-wheel-drives are heavy.'

'Don't want to take the risk. Besides, we need the driver to make sure those ropes don't start to fray.'

Francesca pushed the wet hair out of her eyes. 'Take the risk,' she said grimly. 'I'll drive the Jeep.'

Conrad said, 'Francesca! No.'

She looked at him. She was soaked to the skin. Her hair was plastered to her head. The thunder was making her jump and there were a lot of people she didn't know gathered round to listen. She didn't care. This might be the last chance she ever had. She had to tell him.

'I love you.' She had to shout. She shook back her sodden hair. Her chin tilted with determination. 'And I'm not letting you fall off this bloody mountain if I can help it.'

Conrad looked at her for a long moment.

She met his eyes squarely for all that the rain was spattering her glasses and dripping down her cheekbones. Heedless of the others, she mouthed for him alone, 'I love you.'

She saw him take it in. Welcome it. Then, amazingly, joyously, he laughed. He *laughed*.

She thought: He does love me. A great weight slid off her heart.

'OK,' he called. He sounded like a schoolboy, as if he was actually enjoying this battle with the elements. 'Doctor, on my signal.'

She ran back to the Jeep. She took a moment to check out the unfamiliar. Suddenly she was ice-cold, absorbing details fast and accurately. She would, she knew, most probably have one chance and one chance only. Just as well that she was a boring precision junkie.

She turned on the engine and waved a hand out of the window to tell the doctor she was ready.

There was an almighty crash of thunder right above their heads and lightning snaked down the mountain to their left. Francesca did not even jump. She was wholly concentrated on the doctor, waiting for his signal.

Then Conrad fired up the bus's engine. The doctor's hand dropped. Conrad hauled on the steering wheel. Francesca flung the Jeep into reverse. She felt the drag of the bus and gave it more gas, carefully. This was no time to be panicked into a dash for safety.

There was the horrible groaning of metal. One of the trees to which the bus was secured began to bend. Conrad fought the wheel.

Then there was a crunch and the bus lurched back onto the road. The Jeep began to gather speed. Francesca eased off the gas immediately. She braked and brought the vehicle to a neat stop in the middle of the potholed road.

She sat there, breathing hard. All the danger that she had wiped out of her mind rolled over her in a tidal wave. She began to shake.

Conrad leaped down out of the bus and ran back down the road to her. The rain turned his cotton shirt transparent in seconds. He did not seem to notice. He wrenched open the door.

'Francesca. My darling. My darling.'

He hauled her out of the Jeep into his arms. His mouth on hers was almost savage.

'You're all right. Oh, God, you're all right,' he said, kissing her frantically. His arms were so tight she could hardly breathe but she did not care. 'Thank God you're all right.'

Her embrace was as convulsive as his. She could feel every rib, his shoulder blades and the long, elegant spine as totally as if he were naked in her arms.

'Don't ever do that again,' she scolded.

And began to sob.

'Don't, don't, my darling. Don't cry. There's nothing to cry about. You're safe. I'm safe. Even the damned bus is safe. We're going to be fine.'

But the tears continued to flow.

He looked round helplessly. 'I haven't got one damned thing to dry your eyes.'

Francesca gave a reluctant choke of laughter. 'In this? Who's going to dry anything?'

But it was what she needed. She pulled herself together visibly. Conrad looked at her carefully.

'OK? We have to go on, you know.'

She nodded, sniffing a bit but composed. 'Yes. I'm fine now. Let's get this bus delivered.'

As she sat in the Jeep again, beside the driver, her tears dried on her cheeks. Francesca hardly noticed.

He loves me, she thought. She was half-bewildered, half-exultant. He really, really loves me.

CHAPTER NINE

THEY took the rest of the journey at snail's pace. Even after the thunderstorm passed over and the rain abated the road was still slippery as hell. And there was an occasional rattle as dislodged stones skittered down onto the road or the roofs of the vehicles.

Francesca didn't care. They had survived. And Conrad loved her. The landscape, brilliantly green after its drenching, was the most beautiful she had ever seen. She had never been so happy. .

Everyone came out to greet them in the hilltop village. It was clearly a major ceremony. There was a small brass band and a lot of bunting. Even the parking place for the first-aid bus had been marked out with old oilcans, incongruously swathed in green and gold ribbons.

'The national colours,' explained her driver carelessly. 'From the old days.'

Francesca nodded. But she was not really listening. She was thanking God for Jazz and all her practical advice. Thanks to Jazz, she actually had dry clothes and a hairbrush in her big bag. She did not want to stand on a dais listening to speeches with her damp shirt clinging to her revealingly and a dirty face.

'I need somewhere to change,' she said. 'Fast.'

The driver nodded and slid the Jeep round a steep corner to the back of a single-storey building with a Chinese hat of a roof.

'Church,' he explained.

Francesca slid out and sprinted for the low door, her bag over her shoulder. There was no priest there, but a woman cleaning understood her few words of agitated Montassurran—

and even more agitated gestures—easily enough. She was shown into a tiny room with a loo, a cracked bit of mirror and no washbasin.

'Thank you, Jazz,' muttered Francesca, breaking out the baby wipes.

It took her six minutes to get into the black dress, fluff out her hair and scrub her face and hands clean. Then she took a deep breath, pinned on what she hoped was a princessly smile, and went out to meet the brass band.

And Conrad.

He saw her as soon as she came round the corner. Francesca realised he must have been scanning the village square for her. Her heart warmed. She went to him.

Their hands locked, without either of them losing eye contact. It was like magnetism. They just found each other because it was inevitable. He smiled right into her eyes.

'You look gorgeous.'

'Thank you,' said Francesca demurely. 'So do you.'

It was true, too. The damp shirt outlined musculature that was normally hidden under discreet suiting. But it was not the muscles, not even the damp, springy dark hair. It was that look he had of being brilliantly alive, as if he could not wait to take on the next challenge and the next. She had never seen him look like that.

'Danger must agree with you,' she said.

Unseen, his fingers tightened round her hand. '*You* agree with me.'

She blushed, amused and delighted. Someone took a photograph. And the band straggled into the national anthem. Conrad drew her hand into the crook of his elbow and the welcome celebration was off to a brave start.

It took a long time. Everyone wanted to have their say and some of it was pretty verbose. Thanking heaven for the phrase book and the boring journey when she'd had nothing else to read, Francesca did her best to grope her way after the rapid Montassurran. She gathered that they were grateful for the medical support, grateful for the international attention, glad to welcome Crown Prince Conrad and his friends. There was big applause here and a small girl with a bouquet and hair ribbons had to be prevented from falling off the shaky dais. Conrad grabbed the seat of her embroidered party frock, and Francesca went down on one knee to receive the bouquet.

That was when she saw the small girl's fingers. Someone must have given the child chocolate. Disaster! The dress was eye-hurting white, under the exquisite hand-embroidery. Clearly it was the product of some fond mother's or grand-mother's fine handiwork and laundry. Now it was all set on a collision course with confectionery.

Francesca's heart went out to all concerned. Without think-ing, she grabbed the child's wrists in one hand and whipped out a baby wipe with the other. She eradicated the chocolate in four rapid strokes.

The small girl stood still, regarding the operation with mild interest. But a concerted, 'Aaah,' went up from the small crowd.

Francesca winced. She was not a sugary girl. But she knew her duty. She smiled and held out her hand for the bouquet.

But the small girl had decided she did not want to give it up. There was a little tussle. Then three figures materialised at the side of the dais, hissing instructions. The small girl reluctantly relinquished the flowers. Debated for a minute; looked doubtfully at her mentors; then delivered a butterfly kiss to Francesca's startled cheek.

Francesca nearly overbalanced in surprise.

'No! Curtsey,' hissed the trio of stage managers from the sidelines, in Montassurran agony.

'Don't let her do that,' said Conrad hurriedly. 'They get stuck.'

Swift as a hawk, he swooped on the small girl, swept her up, and handed her down from the dais to her waiting family. The kiss the child gave him was a whole lot more enthusiastic, noticed Francesca, straightening.

There was a ripple of laughter and even some applause.

'Oops,' muttered Francesca. 'I think we just turned into a cliché.'

'Then you shouldn't be so beautiful, my fairy-tale princess,' said Conrad, laughing into her eyes. But there was more than laughter in his voice. There was a deep, deep beckoning. Come with me, it said. Come with me over the horizon to passion unimaginable.

He kissed her hand.

I'm in heaven, she thought. And tonight he will come to me and we will make love as we should have done after Black Conrad's birthday ball. And he will know how much I love him. And I will find out what it is like to have a great lover. She hugged herself, full of tender laughter. And we'll sort out a recovery programme to make sure he is never again a terrible husband.

But, of course, it didn't happen like that.

They only went back to the little mountain town to collect their luggage.

'There's a reception in Vilnagrad tonight,' said Conrad, after talking to some of the men with mobile phones and helicopters. 'We have to go.'

Francesca would have gone to the end of the world with him just then. Vilnagrad was a piece of cake. Except, of course, that among the formalities and the political negotiations—her rudimentary Montassurran gave out at this point—Conrad was locked in meetings deep into the night. At least, she supposed that was why he did not come to her magnificent new apartment in the old palace.

She sat up for a long time, waiting. She had managed to pick up the photographs that the boy had taken of them on their walk last night. So she took a lamp out onto her balcony in the stifling air and riffled through them.

She smiled. All those glossy candid shots that the paparazzi had hidden behind lampposts to get! Here was the truth, taken by a pre-teen amateur on a perfect evening.

Conrad laughing. Conrad chasing her. Conrad throwing weeds at her.

Conrad in love?

She was sure. After the way he had looked at her on the mountain path today, she was positive.

But as the moon rose, and the noise of first the distant city and then the crickets in the bushes died down, she became less and less sure. By the time the owls started to call, she would not have put any money on it at all.

And the next day, though Conrad smiled at her across the parquet reception hall, he did not get to her side. He was wearing his suit again and surrounded by men with mobile phones. She even saw a clipboard. She smiled, but there was a little chill inside her.

She hung onto the belief of that wet road in the thunderstorm. But it got harder. He was busy, she told herself. He was preparing the way for Felix to return for the presidential election. He was organising what should happen to money from the Hospitals Fund.

But... But...

And then he asked if he could come and see her.

It was the end of a hard day's official programme. She had seen the National Museum and the oldest church, newly opened after years of neglect and oppression. She had met officials from the Ministry of Education and visited a brand-new school. She had viewed a display of gymnastics. Toured a vineyard. She saw the famous Montassurran lace being made by intent-faced women sitting in the late-afternoon sun, outside dark cottages on the edge of birch woods. She was drained of appreciative nothings and her feet hurt.

But she jumped up as soon as the double doors opened, her heart in her eyes.

Conrad came in and gave her a quick peck on the cheek. He was in overdrive.

'Haven't got long,' he said rapidly. He had brought his own clipboard. Well, a list, at least. He was making a *list* of things he needed to talk to her about? 'They want us to talk to the Press. Wedding here? Is that OK?'

'What?'

'They want a big display. Round-the-world broadcast. Good for the image. Good for tourism.'

Francesca felt the little chill inside her make a leap. Suddenly it was not little any more.

'Is that what you want?' she said quietly.

'The national income needs it,' he said almost absently. 'Boost the services account.'

The chill had got up somewhere behind her eyes. They felt frozen. She wondered if she would ever be able to close them again.

She said painfully, 'Conrad, we can't get married because it's a boost to the national economy.'

He didn't seem to understand. 'Of course not. But they would really welcome us.'

'We've got to talk about this—'

'And they want to know whether we will live here. I've said no. We're both working people. The country can't afford royals who don't work. But we'll keep a home here and I shall teach one term a year at the university. Sound reasonable?'

He sounded so busy. So practical. So *sensible*. He was turning their private lives into items on a national calendar and he didn't even notice that they had lost the ability to touch each other.

She said casually, 'You know, your grandmother told me you didn't do intimacy.'

'What?' Conrad looked up from his list.

'Never mind.'

He let it go, looking quickly at his watch.

'Now, about your career...'

'I'm not qualified to teach at the university,' Francesca said with irony.

He grinned. 'Maybe not. But you could sure run a kindergarten, judging by your performance yesterday.'

It hurt so much that for a moment she could hardly speak. When she did, she said, 'Oh, I perform well for the camera.'

He frowned. 'Sorry?'

She went to the bureau and produced the boy's photographs.

'Maybe you should put these out. Good for the image, don't you think? Might make that boy his fortune if one of the agencies pick up a couple. Think what that would do for the national income.'

Conrad flipped through them. 'I see what you mean.'

Francesca started to shake. 'Oh, I'm an *asset*,' she said bitterly.

He passed a hand over his brow. 'If you've got a point, make it, Francesca. I haven't got time for guessing games.'

Anger bloomed suddenly. It was almost healing.

'When I said I'd marry you I didn't think I was agreeing to hitch up to a programme of good works and a conference with you a couple of times a week,' said Francesca crisply. 'I want out.'

'What?' He could not have been more astonished if she had threatened to jump out of the window.

She thought *Take me in your arms.*

She said, 'That's not a marriage, Conrad. That's a PR job.'

He looked shaken. 'That's marriage to me.'

It hurt so much she wanted to die. 'So I see. I'm sorry, Conrad. I'm not the woman for the job.'

'But you are,' he said eagerly. 'You're a natural. You've done brilliantly.'

She wanted to scream and throw things. She wanted to crawl into a corner and die. Even now, when he was trying to persuade her to stay with him, he couldn't put his arms round her.

Francesca swallowed and pulled herself together.

'I'm sorry, Conrad. I'm sure you have important stuff to do. But I'm not the person to do it with. I'm calling a halt now.'

He just stared.

She went on with painful quietness, 'I'll fall in with whatever you want to do about announcing it. You choose the timing. Just let me know what you decide.'

He was very pale. 'But—'

Her eyes stung. But she still had her pride. 'It's been a long day. I could really do with a good soak. If you'll forgive me.'

'Francesca—'

'I'm *tired*, Conrad,' she said, her voice breaking.

And he had meetings. And a Press conference that would now need adjusting, she thought ironically. And a presidential candidate for a grandfather to keep informed.

'We'll talk tomorrow,' he promised.

Francesca kept her eyes wide. She nodded. She did not trust her voice.

He said angrily, 'You wanted to come. You must have known what it would be like.'

Her throat hurt. She folded her lips together. 'No. Now I do—I want out.'

He eyed her broodingly. But she did not yield. In the end, he gave up.

'I'll see you tomorrow.'

He went.

The next day she did not see him at all.

But she saw her own publicity. Lots of it. The photograph of her, baby wipe in hand, scrubbing the small girl's fingers had gone round the world, it seemed. Suddenly there were photographers everywhere. Suddenly pictures of her and Conrad were in every paper she ever saw.

Somebody—she prayed it was not Conrad—had passed their sunset romp to a picture agency. *In Love at Last* screamed the headline of a French glossy magazine. It listed the ladies Conrad had escorted before and after his marriage. There were photographs of them. To a woman they were cool and gorgeous and sophisticated. And of course there was Silvia, queenly as a ballerina. He had actually said he was in love with Silvia. Which he never had with her. Francesca's confidence shrank to the size of a pinhead.

She wished she had never seen the article. But someone had kindly got her a copy and delivered it to her room in the official guest house.

The guest house had been the royal palace until the Second World War. She kept coming across sepia photographs of men who could have been Felix's brothers, even one who looked like Conrad.

'Just as well,' said Francesca. 'Or I'd have forgotten what he looks like.'

For days, it seemed, the nearest she got to him was three places away at long formal dinner tables.

Her black dress began to feel tired. But not as tired as she was. Heaven did not last, indeed.

I wish I was at home, she acknowledged to herself in the end.

But it was hopeless. The whole world was in love with the lovers. Felix and Angelika were coming to Vilnagrad to join them. It was a fairy-tale romance for the twenty-first century.

Only, to Francesca, in the middle of it, it felt more like a tragedy.

She stopped looking at the papers. The photographs made Conrad look so happy. So—yes, she had not been fooling herself entirely—in love.

Maybe he had been in love, for that brief moment in time, Francesca thought. But then affairs of state and Felix's bid for the presidency, if her Montassurran was to be relied on, had reminded him of real life. And it had all evaporated, like the smokescreen it was.

She sent him a message. That was what it had come down to. She could not actually walk down the corridor and knock on his door. Hell, she didn't even know where his room was. She had to send a message through her interpreter to the Ministry of Protocol, who would pass it on.

She wrote, 'I've done what I came for. I need to get back. I have things to do in London. Can you arrange it please? Francesca.'

She hesitated a long time over whether or not to put 'love'. But she was not sure what he would do with the note. Maybe he would pass it straight back to one of his official aides to deal with. She did not want to send her love to the Ministry of Protocol.

She did not expect that Conrad would come and see her again. Of course she didn't. He was so busy now. Much busier, she suspected, than he had ever expected to be. But she sort of hoped...

He didn't. He telephoned.

'Hi, Francesca? Conrad.' She could hear people talking in the background, another telephone ringing, the tap of someone working on a laptop keyboard. 'What's this about going home?'

He was clearly surrounded by aides and assistants, all busy, busy. Francesca felt redundant. And lonely. And annoyed with herself. Time to fight back, she thought.

So she said lightly, 'Oh, you know. I've done what I said I would. Now it's time to move on. Places to go. People to see.'

There was a pause. She was almost certain that someone asked him a question and he waved them into a holding pattern.

'You never said you were time-limited.' He sounded put out.

'I never said I'd put my life on hold indefinitely, either,' she flashed.

He said sharply, 'Is this about Barry de la Touche?'

'What?'

'He got himself an interview with *Royal and Swinging Magazine* or whatever the damn thing's called. Said you dumped him for me and his heart is broken. You don't believe that nonsense, do you?'

Francesca seized it like a lifeline, though of course Barry had never loved her. What was more, she had never loved him. She saw that so clearly now that she knew what it was like to be in love.

She could still do with some self-respect, though, she thought wryly. 'Maybe he's had second thoughts.'

'You *can't* be that gullible.' Conrad sounded furious.

Maybe if he had sounded worried... Maybe if he had sounded just the tiniest bit concerned... Maybe if he had not called her gullible...

She could feel the temper coming out of the top of her head. 'No, and I'm not a cipher either. I want out.'

She slammed the phone down before he could answer.

It got her a lot of attention. All of a sudden she had her own aide from the Ministry of Protocol. Several ministers asked to see her. Even ex-King Felix called from London.

She could have screamed, I don't *want* you to make a fuss of me as if I'm a spoilt child. I want Conrad.

She didn't, of course.

In the end he did come himself. He was almost unrecognisable in a grey suit and conservative tie. Well, here was someone who had not let his wardrobe dictate to him, thought Francesca ironically. She was still washing her underwear at night, living off her economical supply of clothes. 'Did you go shopping?' she asked.

For a moment he looked confused. He also, she realised with compunction, looked very tired.

Then he shrugged. 'Oh, someone got it for me, yes.'

Compunction died abruptly. 'Well, bully for you. I'm still juggling between stonewashed jeans and my mother's little black dress.'

He looked impatient. 'Then have them organise you something else. It's not difficult. There are dress shops in Vilnagrad, you know.'

'Have them...!' She was speechless for a moment. 'You know, Conrad, this royalty thing has really gone to your head.'

He had the grace to look a little ashamed. He pushed back his hair with a weary gesture. 'Sorry. It's just that clothes are the least of my worries at the moment.'

She was tempted to ask what his biggest worries were. She nearly did. But then she thought: He could have confided in me any time in the last six days if he wanted. He's known where to find me; which is more than I have known about him. And she hardened her heart.

'Sorry about that. It doesn't matter anyway. I want to get back to London as soon as possible.

He hesitated. 'But I thought you were enjoying yourself.'

'You thought I would fall in love with all that phoney publicity,' spat Francesca, hurt bubbling over at last. 'You thought once I got to be the fairy princess of the international media I'd be so dazzled I'd just go along for the ride. Well, I'm not and I won't.'

'I never—'

'All that stupid, stupid stuff about how I love kids. I don't know a thing about kids. I've never had anything to do with kids.' Her voice rose almost to a scream. 'It's a complete fiction and I'll go mad if I don't get back to where my friends know the truth about me.'

He stared at her, shocked.

'Do you understand?' panted Francesca.

'Yes.' His teeth barely parted as he said it. His voice revealed no emotion at all. 'It was all a fiction. You want to go back to real life. Perfectly clear. I will organise it at once.'

Maybe he did. She did not know. For the next visitor she had—when she got back from a children's entertainment about Black Conrad the hero who freed Montassurro from the invader—was ex-King Felix. Straight from the airport, loaded with suitcases and beaming duplicitously.

'My dear child,' he said, clasping her to his toad-like bosom. 'What a triumph.'

You did not lay out a seventy-five-year-old ex-king with a well-judged lcft hook, even if he was a wily old manipulator who had ruined your life. Francesca extracted herself from his embrace.

'What do you want?' she said wearily.

He became even more avuncular. 'I hear you were worried about not having the right clothes with you.'

'What?'

'That's what Conrad said.'

She did not believe it. Her wardrobe! He really thought she was worried about her *wardrobe*? And then he went and told his horrible old grandfather, Mr Fixit of the Hapsburg Empire. It looked as if she was not the only one who had missed out on the sensitivity gene. How wrong could you get people?

I'll kill him, she thought.

The ex-king did not notice. Clearly insensitivity was inherited.

He swept on, 'And, of course, there's the ball tonight. You won't have brought anything to wear for that. So I just asked your mother and that amusing friend of yours from the bookshop for help. *Et voilà.*'

He waved a hand at the cases.

Francesca stared at him in disbelief. 'You went through my clothes?'

He looked shocked. 'Not I. Your friend Jazz.'

'How dare…?' She broke off abruptly as what he had said caught up with her. 'What ball?'

Felix smiled sunnily. 'Midsummer. St John's Day. Call it what you like. There's always a big civic reception that night. Only this year it will be bigger. I am presenting my grandson to his people.'

Francesca shook her head to clear it. 'You're mad,' she said with conviction. 'This is the twenty-first century, not a Lehar operetta.'

'Not at all. The palace has a wonderful ballroom. The guests were already invited. Well,' he twinkled at her confidingly, 'we have added one or two.'

'I'll bet,' muttered Francesca.

He pretended not to hear that. 'It was all very last-minute. But I have managed to bring over several cases of champagne to drink a toast to the new era of freedom. Also Conrad's uniform. And dresses for you to choose from.'

She said, 'Not me. I'm going home.'

Felix took her hands. She tried to fight him off but he took them anyway. He looked very serious.

'Francesca, my dear. You must listen to me. You have to be there. Conrad needs you.'

She was taken totally off guard. Hopeful, vulnerable, all over again. 'He does?'

'Of course. He is nothing without you.'

She trembled suddenly. 'Did he say so?'

'He does not have to. Everyone knows it.'

'Oh!'

She hugged it to her. He needed her. He was nothing without her. Everyone knew it.

'You are an invaluable asset.'

Francesca tried not to wince. Her smile became a bit fixed, though.

'So friendly. So unaffected. So in love with my Conrad. Believe me, you are the best ambassador we could have chosen.'

She stopped smiling abruptly.

'I had my doubts. I admit it. At first, it did not seem at all hopeful. But this trip—you have been wonderful. Surpassed all our expectations.'

Our expectations! *Our* expectations? Did that include Conrad's expectations?

All of a sudden, Francesca began to feel very cold. She wrapped her arms round herself, though the palace guest room was almost uncomfortably warm in the afternoon sun.

'Oh?' she said dangerously.

But ex-King Felix was on a roll. Anyway, he was not good at recognising danger.

'It is entirely because of you that the curator of the National Museum has agreed to release the crowns.'

Francesca was confused. 'What crowns?' she said, thinking of some mediaeval coins she had seen. 'Why?'

Felix clicked his tongue. 'Well, not my crown. That would be a breach of the constitution. But the crown prince's crown and, of course, a small tiara for you.'

She looked at him, speechless. He began to get an inkling that perhaps he had not played this scene very well.

'It is a great honour,' he said in a reproachful tone.

'Too great for me. I'm going home.'

He was alarmed. There was something, as he afterwards told his wife, so implacable in her tone.

'You can't,'

'Watch me.'

'But...' He was, after all, an experienced diplomat. 'What about Conrad?'

'Conrad's doing just fine without me.'

'But that is the point. He was not doing fine until he had you.'

Francesca looked at him mutinously and said nothing.

Felix thought about all those magazines he had been so gleefully reading the last few days. He said with total sincerity, 'My dear, you have brought him back to his country.'

'I'm happy for him.' She turned away. 'So I'd say my job's done.'

'Not at all. You have brought him happiness such as I have never seen.'

Felix realised it was true suddenly. He sobered, dropping the histrionics.

'I know it's none of my business. But don't walk out on him now. I think perhaps he really does need you.'

Francesca turned and scanned him, narrow-eyed. For the first time since he had arrived he had stopped smiling.

She said slowly, 'You mean that.'

'I have known him a long time. I've never known him to stuff grass down a girl's dress,' said Felix simply. 'Don't let me mess it up for him. For both of you.'

She hesitated.

'Just tonight?' he wheedled. 'Stay tonight, and talk in the morning.'

She still hesitated.

Felix was in despair. 'Don't you want to give him one more chance?'

She still said nothing. He gave up and left.

Alone, Francesca went to the window and looked out at the formal gardens. The palace was not large but the gardens had everything you would expect—fountains, clipped hedges, neat geometric beds of roses and well-raked paths. She did not see any of them.

Did she want to give Conrad one last chance? Did she?

And out of her memory came his voice, warm with laughter and friendship; yet still with that unmistakeable undertow of sexuality, pulling her, pulling her, towards the open seas of passion.

Then you shouldn't be so beautiful, my fairy-tale princess.

They had nearly had their idyll. So nearly.

She shivered uncontrollably. Oh, yes, she wanted to give Conrad one last chance. She wanted to give it to them both.

More than wanted. Needed.

'If there's a chance that he loves me,' Francesca said aloud, 'I'll risk anything.'

CHAPTER TEN

OF COURSE, that meant risking wearing a tiara, which Francesca had not quite been prepared for. Later that evening she sat in front of the mirror in her room and watched gloomily as the pretty diamond headdress lurched inexorably towards her left ear.

'I have the wrong hair. The wrong-shaped head. I keep moving. I don't know what it is. I just can't wear this thing,' she said to the woman from the Montassurran Ministry of Culture in despair.

'The Ministry of Culture cannot help. No one has ever worn it in living memory,' said the other with sympathy. 'Perhaps hairgrips? Hair spray? Gel?'

'Perhaps chewing gum and cement,' muttered Francesca.

But in the end she wedged it into place and kept it there. At least, as long as she took very small steps and did not turn her head too fast. She hoped vengefully that Conrad was having similar trouble with the crown prince's headgear.

But when they met in the mirror-panelled ante-room, before their long-delayed Press conference, Conrad was not wearing any sort of crown. His dark hair was shiny and newly washed. How come I know that he got out of the shower less than twenty minutes ago? thought Francesca, with a little shiver of longing. And totally crown-free.

On the other hand, he was wearing narrow white trousers with a gold stripe down the side, a green and gold tunic with gold trimmings and epaulettes, and a sword. And a frosty expression. Francesca suddenly felt a lot more cheerful.

'Hi. Do you sing tenor or baritone?' She gestured at the tunic. 'Love the jacket. Don't tell me. The national colours.'

Conrad's expression did not lighten. 'The uniform of the Mountain Hussars. I drew the line at spurs.'

He didn't love her. Probably. He had used her and he wanted to go on using her. Certainly. And he thought of her as an asset, possibly saleable. But he still looked gorgeous in his musical-comedy uniform. And he *hated* it.

Francesca could have laughed aloud but didn't. She still had that self-respect to regain.

'Just thank God you've got the butt for it,' she advised crisply. 'Felix would look like the Michelin man in that get-up.'

Conrad's lip curled. 'Are you by any chance thinking of me as a sex object?' He sounded disgusted.

Francesca hid a grin. 'Yup.'

He gave her a sudden, wicked sideways look under his lashes. 'Excellent. That's the most hopeful thing I've heard all week. Keep up the good work.'

Francesca choked.

The Press conference was an ordeal. She had got her briefing. The notes were on the table in front of her. But if she looked down the bloody tiara would almost certainly fall over her eyes. So Francesca concentrated on keeping her answers as short as possible and batting anything difficult in Conrad's direction.

So she heard him say that, yes, he was glad to have brought medical supplies to Montassurro and to have seen so much of the country he had not known before. Yes, and Francesca would continue to work for the Montassurran Hospital Fund. No, he was not intending to take part in Montassurran politics. Yes, he would continue to work as a seismologist.

'Here?' asked one journalist.

'Possibly. Why do you think I was always so interested in earthquakes? Montassurro has had so many over the centuries. Maybe there is a Carpathian fault line we don't know about yet.'

Would he ever seek the throne?

No.

Would he ever take the throne if it was offered?

'Unlikely. But I'd have to ask my wife. It's not a decision a married man could take on his own.'

There was a chorus of sympathetic endorsement. Crown Prince Conrad was proving what a right-on new man he was, thought Francesca, her ire reigniting. If it wouldn't have dislodged the tiara, she could have thrown things.

Their questioning turned to her. Now here comes the schmaltz, thought Francesca, wincing.

'Look,' she said. 'Every single journalist in this room has seen a picture of me wiping a child's chocolatey fingers. So you all decided that I'm the angel in the house. I'm here to tell you, that's not me. I'm a bookseller. I've got a clever friend with a strategy that embraces sticky fingers. I take advice. That's all.'

There was a chorus of laughter.

She said seriously, 'I mean this. I've had a lot of fun and I've learned a lot in Montassurro. But I'm no mother-of-the-nation in the making. And Conrad's career choices are up to him.'

They left to applause.

In the corridor outside he said, 'Thanks for staying on. We made a good team.' A pause. 'As usual.'

She stared straight ahead. Well, it kept the tiara in place. So she was not looking at him when she said, 'In public.'

He stopped dead. 'What?'

She kept on walking. 'I mean, the teamwork is strictly for public consumption. You're a tactician. And I'm an *asset*.' Her voice bit. 'So you use me. That's what assets are for, isn't it?'

He caught up with her. 'You can't believe that.' He sounded stunned.

'No? So I'm not an asset?'

'Yes, of course you are.' He was impatient. 'But you're a lot more than that. You have to know that.'

'I don't,' said Francesca, approaching the ballroom at a rate of knots. 'And I still want to go home as soon as the fuss dies down.'

Conrad lengthened his stride. Behind them the aides broke into a trot.

'But I love you.'

She spun on her heel to face him. The tiara lurched dangerously. Francesca ignored it.

'Prove it,' she flung at him.

He said thoughtfully, 'I think that had better come off, don't you?'

He eased the tiara out of its fixings, then ran his fingers through her disarranged hair tenderly.

'That's not proof,' said Francesca with disgust. 'That's marketing.'

His eyes lit with laughter. 'You've set me a real puzzler there,' he said as if he was agreeing with something she had said. 'Quite a challenge.'

One of the aides caught up with them. Conrad handed him the tiara without looking at either the man or the diamonds. 'Get that back to the museum, will you, Tony? Miss Heller only has to sneeze and it will fly off and blind someone.'

'Yes, Your Highness,' said Tony, grinning.

'So we're all ready to go in? Even my grandfather?'

'Yes, Your Highness.'

And, indeed, there was Felix, more subdued than Conrad, in a black suit only relieved by an impressive double row of medals. The prime minister, who joined them, only had a single row, Francesca saw. She was almost certain that Felix had seen it too and was gleeful.

But she didn't care about Felix. Conrad had not answered her challenge. She watched him as an aide chivvied them into a line based on some sort of obscure protocol.

'It's like kindergarten,' she said under her breath to Conrad. 'I shall never get the hang of it. What are you going to do?'

'About my credibility gap?' He was thoughtful. 'I'm not sure yet. Interesting. But first I've got to escort Mrs Prime Minister in to dinner and try and curb Felix's determination to offer himself up to be crowned.'

She winced, remembering that overheard conversation all those weeks ago.

'I know. You don't like human sacrifice.'

But in his grandmother's kitchen Conrad had been saying he wouldn't let Felix force him into marrying her.

He looked amused. 'And you, daughter of your father, don't let go of grudges.'

He touched her cheek so fleetingly that Francesca was half-convinced she had imagined it. Except she jumped like a grasshopper whenever he touched her, no matter how lightly.

He smiled caressingly. 'Don't worry, my darling. I'll think of a way to convince you.'

The dinner was interminable and the dancing an ordeal. The honoured guests, Francesca found, were supposed to file out in an orderly fashion, unified as they had arrived. So by the time Felix indicated that he was ready to leave she could have screamed with frustration. Conrad was so close, just three seats away from her, yet as inaccessible as the moon.

And as soon as they were outside the ballroom Felix put a hand on the green military sleeve and said, 'Walk me to my room. I need to talk to you.'

They both bade Francesca an absent goodnight and hurried off.

She went back to her room and kicked embroidered footstools. Then she packed, with vicious movements. Then she cleaned her teeth so violently she sprayed the bathroom mirror with a fine peppermint mist and nearly made herself choke.

Then she flung herself into bed and tried to sleep. It was hopeless. Every time she closed her eyes she found herself composing her final devastating annihilation of Crown Prince Conrad Domitio.

And then the shutters started banging. She bounced up in bed.

'This is too much.'

She swung her feet out of bed and steamed across the elderly Aubusson to the tall windows and sprang the catch before marching out onto the balcony.

'Damn fancy Hapsburg architecture,' she muttered, grabbing the loose shutter and walking it back to the wall. 'Why didn't they make their shutter guards solid?'

'Why indeed?' said an amused voice.

Francesca nearly fell off the balcony. The shutter swung wide with her attached to it. Conrad caught her in one strong arm, and shouldered the shutter back into place. He flicked the iron hook into its restraint and smiled down at her.

'Wh-what are you doing here?'

'I had an inspiration,' he said coolly. And tipped her off her feet entirely.

'Whaa-aagh,' said Francesca unromantically but with feeling. She clutched him convulsively. 'Put me down. I'm too heavy.'

'Too heavy for what?' he asked, interested.

She found she was blushing to her eyebrows in the night air.

But she said with asperity, 'Too heavy for silly games.'

Conrad laughed. 'I don't think so.'

He stepped round the French windows and took her back to the rumpled bed.

'Couldn't sleep, I see,' he said with satisfaction.

And tipped her on top of the covers.

Francesca stared up at him. She was wearing an old much-washed T-shirt and nothing else. She had never felt more at a disadvantage in her life.

She spat, 'Don't you dare laugh at me.'

'Who's laughing?'

He kissed her. He was hot and hungry and absolutely certain of what he was doing. Francesca, who did not reckon herself inexperienced, thought she had never encountered assurance like this. Or—she had to admit—hunger.

It was her hunger too. Her heat. She arched up to him, dragging him into her arms fiercely. Her response was unequivocal. Conrad's loving was like forest fire—breathless, out of control, *devastating*. He kissed her throat, her breasts, her long, smooth thighs. Her T-shirt hit the wall, flung with a forceful hand, along with his own clothes. Francesca gave a shiver of mingled pleasure and anticipation.

And then he gathered her up against him and she began to tease him. Her body was made for this. Somehow, she did not know how, she knew this man. Something deep in the core of her recognised his every reaction, every held breath, every half-muffled groan. She pushed him back and began to taste his skin, luxuriating in her power to make him respond.

'Francesca!'

The hard naked body shook with near unbearable need. She ran her hands along the muscled back, the narrow athlete's hips, the tense buttocks and felt rather than heard him gasp. His desire flowed through her hands to her heart. As if it were her own.

'For me?' She was humbled suddenly.

He gave a little laugh that was half a groan of need. 'Who else?'

The words pierced her. Suddenly his desire became hers too. She wanted all her fantasies fulfilled and she wanted to fulfil his. She told him so, her voice ragged.

'Darling.' He brushed the hair off her face. His hand was not quite steady. 'I thought you were never going to want me.'

She sucked in her breath, fiercely brave suddenly. 'I want you.'

It was a harsh first lovemaking. Both were too close to the edge for the luxury of the long, languid wooing that Francesca learned afterwards Conrad was master of. But that first time he was too aware of how close he had come to losing her. And she was too astonished.

They tore into each other like adolescents. Their climax, when it came, was thunderous.

Afterwards, lying in abandon, with his hand clasped to her left breast, he said lazily, 'Convinced at last?'

Francesca turned her head on the pillow and found he was smiling straight into her eyes. Into her heart. She realised she was smiling back. In fact, her whole body was smiling.

'Totally,' she said, stretching.

He lifted himself on one elbow, kissing her breast lingeringly.

'No more doubts?'

'None.'

'Then—for the last time—you will marry me?' He lifted his head and said softly, 'For real.'

Francesca widened her eyes at him mischievously. 'It gets more real than this?'

But Conrad did not laugh. Instead he brushed his thumb backwards and forwards across her sensitised lower lip. Her eyelids quivered in undisguisable response.

'A whole lot.'

'How?' she gasped, lips parting as she felt a hot need rise again. Her limbs began to shift restlessly.

He held off, watching her desire build. 'For richer, for poorer. In sickness and in health,' he whispered. 'That's real for you.'

Francesca could not bear it any more. She lifted towards him. Her head drifted sideways until she was leaning into his chest. It was a gesture as old as time. It said, I love you. I trust you. I'm yours.

'Please,' she sighed.

He kissed her parted lips with exquisite gentleness. 'With my body I thee worship,' he said softly. 'You'll never regret this, Francesca. I promise.'

And proved it.

EPILOGUE

THEY were married three times. Once at a quiet ceremony in the small church in her mother's Cotswold village. Lady Anne and Peter Heller were pleased, of course. But they had largely lost interest in organising their only daughter's marital affairs. They were busy renegotiating their own.

Once in the City Hall of Vilnagrad, with Felix and a smug ex-Queen Angelika as witnesses. They had a Vilnagrad apartment by that time and were well on the way to dual nationality. But neither was giving up their job and the politicians were relieved to know that, unlike his grandfather, Conrad was planning nothing more than extended visits to the country of his ancestors.

'Basically we are like any other newly married couple. We need our privacy,' Conrad told them. 'But we'll do any formal occasions you want. Within reason.' Adding with a wicked look, 'My wife was born to wear a tiara.' The assistant to the Minister of Culture had a coughing fit.

And once, to the sound of bells and some truly amazing brass bands—attended by more photographers than a Hollywood première—in the Cathedral of San Simeone.

'It's just as well I'm used to cameras now,' said Francesca, getting into the gold-emblazoned barouche that the National Museum had lent them for the occasion. She tucked her fairy-tale white figured satin skirts out of the way of the door.

'You're not used to tiaras, though,' said her husband, straightening the diadem tenderly. 'Drive on,' he added to the coachman.

But Francesca was looking back at the crowd on the cathedral steps. 'Hang on, Felix wants something. He's beckoning. Look.'

Conrad cast an uninterested look in his grandfather's direction. 'Ignore him. He's practising a regal wave. Don't take any notice. It only encourages him.'

Francesca saw that he was right. She laughed. 'The old mountebank.'

'Well, he's going to be good for the tourist industry, at least,' said Conrad. He put his arm around her. 'Speaking of which, we'd better do some waving of our own.'

She leaned against his shoulder, warm with love and confidence. And felt the tell-tale slip of a hairgrip.

'Damn. There goes the tiara again. Oh, well, I suppose it will give the papers something to write about.'

She could feel the laughter well up in him.

'I think we can do better than that,' said Conrad coolly.

Under the cover of the long, long kiss that delighted every romantic in the world he whispered, 'You are everything I never thought I was entitled to. I didn't know it was possible to be this happy.'

Francesca glowed. 'This is the best day of my life.'

Conrad's eyelids drooped, in that familiar look of wicked teasing. 'So far,' he drawled. 'So far.'

Modern Romance™
...seduction and
passion guaranteed

Tender Romance™
...love affairs that
last a lifetime

Sensual Romance™
...sassy, sexy and
seductive

Blaze
...sultry days and
steamy nights

Medical Romance™
...medical drama on
the pulse

Historical Romance™
...rich, vivid and
passionate

27 new titles every month.

*With all kinds of Romance for
every kind of mood...*

MILLS & BOON®

FREE
2 BOOKS
AND A SURPRISE GIFT!

We would like to take this opportunity to thank you for reading this Mills & Boon® book by offering you the chance to take TWO more specially selected titles from the Tender Romance™ series absolutely FREE! We're also making this offer to introduce you to the benefits of the Reader Service™ —

- ★ FREE home delivery
- ★ FREE monthly Newsletter
- ★ FREE gifts and competitions
- ★ Exclusive Reader Service discount
- ★ Books available before they're in the shops

Accepting these FREE books and gift places you under no obligation to buy; you may cancel at any time, even after receiving your free shipment. Simply complete your details below and return the entire page to the address below. **You don't even need a stamp!**

YES! Please send me 2 free Tender Romance books and a surprise gift. I understand that unless you hear from me, I will receive 4 superb new titles every month for just £2.55 each, postage and packing free. I am under no obligation to purchase any books and may cancel my subscription at any time. The free books and gift will be mine to keep in any case.

N2ZEC

Ms/Mrs/Miss/Mr ....Initials ....
BLOCK CAPITALS PLEASE

Surname ....

Address ....

....

....Postcode ....

Send this whole page to:
UK: FREEPOST CN81, Croydon, CR9 3WZ
EIRE: PO Box 4546, Kilcock, County Kildare (stamp required)

Offer valid in UK and Eire only and not available to current Reader Service subscribers to this series. We reserve the right to refuse an application and applicants must be aged 18 years or over. Only one application per household. Terms and prices subject to change without notice. Offer expires 30th September 2002. As a result of this application, you may receive offers from other carefully selected companies. If you would prefer not to share in this opportunity please write to The Data Manager at the address above.

Mills & Boon® is a registered trademark owned by Harlequin Mills & Boon Limited.
Tender Romance™ is being used as a trademark.